SEALED WITH A LOVING KISS
and other stories

ABOUT WRITING WEST MIDLANDS

Writing West Midlands is the literature development agency for the West Midlands region of the UK. We run events and activities for writers and readers, including our annual Birmingham Literature Festival. We also run Spark Young Writers, which is a major programme of work for young writers aged 8 to 16+ including regular workshops, a summer

school and a magazine. Writing West Midlands also works with libraries, publishers and universities to help creative writers develop their skills.

ABOUT READ ON

READ ON is a major Creative Europe funded project across six European countries working in five

languages. It aims to encourage young people aged 12 to 19 to engage with reading and creative writing. Writing West Midlands is the UK partner. Work taking place in the West Midlands includes creative writing workshops, a young presenters scheme as part of the Birmingham Literature Festival and training sessions on vlogging and podcasting. The *After Summer* anthology has been produced as part of READ ON.

SEALED WITH A LOVING KISS

& Other Stories

COPYRIGHT

Co-funded by the
Creative Europe Programme
of the European Union

Contents

The Missing Peace

Liam Brown

Have you ever noticed how noisy the world is? I'm not just talking about the obvious sounds. The gravelly hack of stop-start traffic. The rattling roar of the wind in the trees. The groan and clank of the bin lorry that stops outside your bedroom window at six o'clock every Tuesday morning. No. I mean the other noises. The ones that fade into the background most of the time. Don't believe me? Try closing your eyes right now and listening. Go on, do it. Don't worry, I'll wait.

Back? Good. So, what did you hear? I'll tell you what I heard as I sat in my office and typed these words.

I heard the hoot of an owl. The spluttering bark of next door's dog. The blare of police sirens and the drip-drip-splat of the broken gutter I've never quite got around to fixing. The distant murmur of a passenger jet. And, closer still, there's the relentless tut of the clock. The low hum of my electric lamp. The stuffy snuffle of my own breath. The clatter and chatter of my sticky keyboard keys. All of these noises, sound after sound, piling up on each other, layer by layer, to create a discordant cacophony that echoes endlessly around my brain, getting louder and louder and louder.

It's enough to drive you completely and utterly crazy...

One person who definitely understood how noisy the world could be was Taz.

Now, if I were to show you a photograph of Taz and ask you what you saw, you might describe a tall, slender girl, fifteen or sixteen years old, with shoulder-length brown hair and a warm, welcoming smile. If you were being particularly observant, you might also point out the archaeological textbook tucked under her arm, or even the younger girl in the corner of photo. The one pulling faces behind her back.

If I were then to ask you what you thought Taz was like, you'd probably reach for a set of fairly obvious adjectives. Happy, you might say. Funny, maybe. Kind. Or, if you'd spotted the dark smudges under her eyes and the ragged tips of her fingernails, you might think that she looked tired. A touch worn out, perhaps. But, that aside, you'd probably agree that Taz looked more or less cheerful and worry-free.

And that's where you'd be wrong. It's true that Taz was capable of being many of those things – happy, kind, warm, welcoming – but the day this photo was taken she was feeling unbelievably stressed out, because she was studying for her end-of-year exams. Or rather, she was trying to study for her exams. You see, ever since she was young, Taz had always wanted to be an archaeologist. She pictured herself discovering dinosaurs in the deserts of Djibouti (the Tazosaurus?) or trekking through a rain-forest in Rio De Janeiro, uncovering the ruins of some hitherto-unknown civilisation. It was her dream job. And if she was to stand any chance of actually realising that dream, she needed to pass her exams. Which meant revising. Unfortunately, Taz was finding that next to impossible.

The problem was her family. Or, specifically, the noise they made every time she took out her books. Seriously, they never shut up, not even for a minute. Every time she attempted to memorise the capital cities of West African countries, or remember how to calculate the angles in an isosceles triangle, her family would start up with the most terrific racket, making it utterly impossible for her to concentrate. Her dad, for example, seemed incapable of talking on the phone without yelling at the top his voice, punctuating every sentence with a great, honking laugh, not unlike a goose playing a broken saxophone. Taz was amazed the neighbours hadn't been round to com-plain. Her mum, meanwhile, seemed to wait until she was settled at her desk with all her books out before she decided to undertake some elaborate DIY task around the house. Drilling, sawing, hitting things with a hammer. It was ridiculous.

It was her younger sister though, who was the most annoying. She was constantly whistling or coughing, or sneezing, or yawning, all of which set Taz's teeth on edge. Even the sound of her eating breakfast cereal was enough to drive her crazy.

More than anything, Taz longed for a whole day to herself where she could revise without the constant banging, stomping and clanging. She daydreamed of desert islands. Of remote mountain tops. Of underground nuclear bunkers. Anywhere that was quiet.

It all came to a head one bright Saturday morning. Taz awoke in a terrible mood. The birds singing outside her window made her want to go on a killing spree. In the bathroom, the sound of her sister brushing her teeth felt like a personal attack. Downstairs, the rumble of the vacuum cleaner seemed to reverberate through her skull. There was no way she was going to get any work done.

But then something miraculous happened. Her family went shopping, leaving Taz alone in the house. Eager to take advantage of the peace, Taz ran up to her room, took out her books and spread them out on her desk. She was feeling a little chilly, so she fetched her cosiest cardigan. Then she decided the wooden chair was a little uncomfortable, so she moved all her books from her desk to her bed. Finally she was ready.

She shut her eyes for a moment. Took a deep breath. Listened. There were no loud telephone conversations. No noisy DIY projects. No jabbering sister. Even the stupid birds had shut their beaks for once. It was the quietest the house had been in months. It was perfect…

Wham!

Taz opened her eyes to the sound of the front door slamming. She was lying face down on her bed, one of her textbooks stuck to her face. She must have fallen asleep. Downstairs, she could hear the familiar chattering and chuntering of her family. Then suddenly an agonised shriek rang out. Had somebody taken her family hostage? Had they been set upon by a pack of wild cheetahs?

Taz sprinted downstairs, ready to save them. As she burst into the living room she was confronted by the sight of her dad clutching a microphone, desperately trying to keep up with the song lyrics that were flickering across the TV screen.

'Hey Taz! Look what we bought,' her sister beamed. 'A karaoke machine.'

It was the final straw. Taz turned around and stormed back up the stairs, slamming her bedroom door behind her. She couldn't take it anymore. Not this house. Not these people. And not this unrelenting noise. She had to leave. Right now.

And so, stuffing her textbooks into her bag, she went over to the window. Then, just as her dad's falsetto echoed out around the house, she slid the window open and proceeded to climb down the drainpipe.

Over the next few hours, Taz worked her way across various locations in the city, trying and failing to find somewhere suitable to revise. There was the local library, closed due to cuts. There was a coffee shop with its overly-chatty barista and the cappuccino machine that sounded like a plane taking off. There was the fast food restaurant with its sizzling griddles and bubbling deep fat fryers. There was the supermarket café, with its bleeping check-outs and squeaky-wheeled trolleys. She even tried a park bench, but in the end the hollering footballers and scream-ing children were too much to handle.

By now, the day was wearing on. She decided to aban-don the city altogether, hopping onto a number 61 bus and staring out of the window as it slowly ground its way through the heaving Saturday traffic. As she sat there, she gradually became aware of the sounds on the bus around her. The crunch and growl of the old diesel engine. The inane chat of the other passengers. The intermittent ring-ing of the bell. The burble of a baby in a buggy. The honk-ing of horns. The clinking of coins. The rasp of the ticket dispenser…

The more she listened, the more difficult it was to tune things out. She felt suffocated by sound. Swaddled. Swamped. And so, without stopping to see where she was, she got up and dived through the doors.

Once she had caught her breath, Taz looked around. She was standing next to a huge field with something bright and glittering in the distance. A group of strange-looking buildings behind a long steel fence. She headed straight for them.

She was perhaps halfway across the field when she realised it was a fairground. The red and white tower of a helter-skelter looking out over dozens of classic rides and games. The waltzer, the dodgems, hook-a-duck, the coconut shy...

Taz's heart sank. If there was one place that was guaranteed to be noisy it was a funfair. And yet, as she drew nearer, she noticed the whole place was oddly subdued. There was no pumping techno music blaring from the rides. No screaming visitors or shouting touts. In fact, the whole place looked completely deserted. As she reached the fence, she saw the reason why. A large banner hung from one of the trailers:

Blippo's Fair, it said, and then underneath that someone had scrawled in permanent marker: Closed until further notice.

Taz pressed her face to the mesh fence. There was no one anywhere. The whole place really did seem to be abandoned. She walked along the fence, peering in at the empty fairground, until she reached the entrance. But there too the ticket booth was unmanned.

'Hello?' Taz called out.

When no one replied, she tried again, this time cupping her hands to her mouth and shouting: 'HELLO?'

On the far side of the park there was a beating of wings, as a flight of grey pigeons took to the sky. Apart from that, there was nothing.

Taz turned back to the fairground. Even though she knew it was probably a terrible idea, the thought of finally having somewhere she could work undisturbed was too tempting to pass up. And so, with a final look over her shoulder, she crept past the deserted ticket office and made her way inside.

When she was younger, Taz had always adored the fair. There was something both thrilling and slightly terrifying about the rides. The way they never felt totally bolted together properly, as if at any moment the pirate ship might detach from its frame and launch off into the neon-stained night air.

Being at the fair during the day was different, though. It was like when the lights at the cinema came up at the end of the film and you were left staring around at the popcorn-scattered floor. Looking around at the motionless rides now, Taz felt a similar sense of disappointment. Without the crowds or the flashing lights, everything just looked sad and ordinary. The faded paintwork. The rusting machinery. The peeling signs. It was as if all the magic had drained away.

As she walked deeper into the fair, Taz began to look for somewhere to sit down and study. Most of the stalls had their shutters pulled down. The rifle range. Whack-a-mole. Tin Can Alley. All of them were closed. She thought for a moment about trying the Hall of Mirrors, before she spotted a ghost train on the far side of the park.

The ride was designed to look like a creepy castle, with a giant painting of Dracula looming over the top of the turrets. As a child, Taz had always been a bit freaked out by the ghost train. Approaching it in the daylight however, she thought the castle looked more like her nan's retirement home. As for Dracula, his white shirt and slicked black hair reminded her of the waiter at her local Italian restaurant. Which is to say, it wasn't very spooky at all. Still, it looked like a perfect spot to study for an hour or two, with more than enough room for her to sit down and spread out her books on the train that was parked in front of the ride.

Just as Taz was climbing into the front carriage, she saw a flutter of movement out of the corner of her eye. She jerked her head up, her heart hammering in her chest. Looking around though, she saw nothing. Only the same deserted fairground that had always been there. She let out a little laugh, shaking her head at how jumpy she was being. Daylight or not, it seemed the ghost train still had the power to unnerve her.

She was about to reach for her bag when she was deafened by a sudden blast of organ music. She looked up in confusion to see the steel bar lowering over her lap before the ride lurched into life, shunting forward so violently that she was forced to cling onto the bar.

'Wait!' she yelled. 'Stop! I want to get off!'

It was no good, though. There was no one there, the ticket booth remaining resolutely empty. The ride was going whether she liked it or not.

Seconds later, the castle doors slid open. And then she was hurtling forwards, disappearing into the darkness.

It took Taz's eyes a moment to adjust to the dim light. To her relief, she saw the ghost train was just as unscary inside as it looked from the front. A robotic spider with seven legs scuttled unconvincingly across a web. A Day-Glo green skeleton popped up from behind a crumpled cardboard gravestone. A couple of rubber bats dangled harmlessly from a wire. Even her little sister wouldn't have been scared by this stuff. If anything, it was just annoying, especially the jaunty organ music that crackled from the speakers at ear-splitting volume. Gritting her teeth, Taz sat back and waited for the ride to be over.

As the train continued its journey, Taz became vaguely aware that the castle was divided into different themes. There was a Western section, where skeletons in Stetsons came busting through swinging saloon doors, pistols twizzling on the ends of their boney index fingers. There was an Ancient Egyptian zone, too – an Andrex-wrapped mummy springing from a papier-mâché sarcophagus.

She had just entered a rather confusing pirate-themed area, where a troupe of animatronic zombie buccaneers were swinging their cutlasses in her direction, when the lights went out completely, and she was plunged into darkness.

For a moment, she dared to hope it was part of the ride. Just another cringey attempt to scare her. Seconds later though, the music cut out and the train shuddered to a stop.

Taz waited in the dark, expecting that at any moment the lights would flash back on and the ride would start up again. A few minutes later, though, there was still no sign of movement. More irritated than frightened, she reached for her bag, feeling around until she found her phone. In the harsh white beam of her torchlight, the zombie pirates looked even more pathetic, the wires and circuitry that powered them easily visible. Taz rolled her eyes. Just then, she spotted something scuttling fast across the floor, followed by a disconcerting squeak. Was that a… rat?

She had no time to think about it, as seconds later there was another, even more alarming noise. The slap and scrape of footsteps, echoing around the castle.

And getting closer by the second.

Taz turned in her seat until her torchlight picked out a figure in the distance. Someone was walking down the tracks towards her. Or rather, something was walking down the tracks. Because, as impossible as it seemed, the figure approaching her appeared to be a clown, a creepy red smile spread across his chalk-white face.

Now Taz was scared. She was terrified. She gripped the steel bar that pinned her knees, desperately trying to force it up, but it wouldn't budge. She was trapped. She looked back up to face the clown, who was almost on her now, his yellow teeth flashing, his eyes wide with anger.

'No! Please!' Taz screamed. 'Stop. STOP!'

To her surprise, the clown did stop. Standing in front of the train, he put his hands on his hips and let out a laugh. Not the blood-curdling, demonic howl Taz was expecting, but rather a soft chuckle. As if he were amused by the sight of her.

'Please don't kill me,' Taz managed to gasp.

The clown looked confused. 'Kill you? What on earth are you talking about? I'm here to rescue you.'

'Rescue me?'

'Yes. From the train. It's been playing up for weeks now. Faulty wiring, I'm afraid. Stops and starts of its own accord. Like it's got a mind of its own. You're lucky I spotted you on the CCTV monitor. I'd like to know what you were thinking, getting on it in the first place. I could report you to the police for trespassing, you know. Although from the looks of it, you've had more than enough of a fright for one day. Now come on, let's get you out of here…'

Once he had freed her from the malfunctioning ride, the clown – who it turned out was called Blippo – led Taz down the track towards safety. As they walked, Taz told the clown about her miserable day, and the difficulty she'd had finding somewhere quiet to study.

'The last place you want to be is a funfair,' Blippo said. 'Although you might have noticed that this one is a little quieter than most. We've had a little issue with… unwanted visitors. Specifically of the four-legged, squeaky variety, I'm afraid. Environmental Protection has shut us down. Temporarily, I might add.'

At last they reached the end of the track, and Taz and the clown emerged from the castle, blinking in the daylight.

'I suppose I'd better be heading off,' Taz said, sheepishly. 'I'm sorry again for causing you so much trouble.'

'Whoa there,' Blippo said. 'Wait up a sec. I've had a

thought. About your noise problem. In fact, I might just have the perfect place for you to study...'

The ride was called The Cosmonaut Experience, and Blippo assured her it was the only one of its kind outside of Japan.

'My son convinced me to buy it. It's the future, he reckons. Though I'm not so sure. You can't beat a good old-fashioned rollercoaster, if you ask me. Still, I have to admit it was pretty popular with the younger crowd. Or at least, it was before blinking Pest Control shut us down.'

'But what is it exactly?' Taz asked.

They were standing outside a small ride that had been designed to look like a space shuttle, the letters NASA painted on the side in red. All of the windows were sealed up, making it impossible to see inside.

'It's a simulator,' Blippo explained. 'A virtual-thingy. You know, like a giant video game. It's pretty good actually. Proper convincing. You can run a number of programmes on it, too. Normally we stick to one called Martian Madness. You're an explorer who's been sent to Mars and then you accidentally stumble into an asteroid belt and... Well, you get the picture. But we have another one too. It's called Lost in Space.'

'Lost in Space? What happens in that one?'

'What do you think happens? Anyway, you'll see for yourself in a minute...'

Before she knew it, Taz was being led up the steps and through the double doors, which hissed as they opened, like an airlock. Inside, she found herself standing in a small room that had been designed to look like the cockpit of a shuttle, only with a huge video screen where the windscreen should be. Blippo strapped Taz into a chair before pressing a couple of buttons on the vast bank of controls in front of her.

'You can stay here as long as you like,' he said. 'It's not like anyone is going to be queuing up to use it.'

And with that, he was gone.

There was a countdown from the tower.

Ten, nine, eight...

And then they were off, blasting up through the atmosphere towards the unknown.

The noise was overwhelming, the whole pod rocking and shaking as the shuttle's rockets roared behind her. Even though Taz knew it was only a simulation, she still gripped her seat tightly. This was scarier than anything she'd seen on the ghost train – even Blippo!

Yet just as soon had it started, the sound of the engine dropped away, leaving Taz staring at a screen full of glittering stars. It was beautiful.

Not only that: it was totally silent.

She reached into her bag and took out her books. Finally, she had found somewhere she could revise in peace.

Yet as the minutes ticked by, something strange happened. As she drifted through the vast, silent cosmos, Taz found it increasingly difficult to concentrate on the words in her books. There was a strange feeling in the pit of her stomach that kept distracting her. At first, she thought it was hunger. For a while, she even wondered if she might be getting sick. But then it struck her.

She was lonely.

Here she was floating through the virtual universe, all alone, while back on the very real Earth, her family were probably going out of their minds with worry.

And so, without even waiting for the shuttle to make its return voyage, she stuffed her books into her bag, undid her straps and headed for the emergency exit.

It was almost dark by the time she finally made it back onto her street. Next door, it sounded as if the neighbours were having some kind of party, cries of excitement and loud music spilling from their open windows. Taz didn't care. She was just happy to be home. Squeezing her way down the back alley and into the garden, she clambered up the drainpipe and swung herself through her open bedroom window.

Once inside, she stopped and listened.

There was nothing. No music. No terrible singing.

Her heart sank. She was too late. Her parents must have noticed she was missing and headed to the police station. They were probably frantic by now.

Flinging open her door, she thundered down the stairs. When she reached the living room, she was amazed to find her family all sitting there, each with a book open on their lap.

'Oh hello, dear,' her mum whispered, looking up. 'Have you finished for the day?'

Taz stared at her, bewildered. 'Finished?'

'Yes. Your sister told us you were busy revising. I'm so sorry if we disturbed you earlier. We thought we'd better keep it down for the rest of the day.'

'Are you kidding?' Taz laughed. 'I don't mind you making noise. You can be as loud as you like.'

With that, she went over to the karaoke machine and picked up a microphone. 'Right then? Who fancies a duet? Dad?'

For the rest of the night, the four of them sang their hearts out. They screeched. They wailed. They hooted and they howled, murdering song after song with their out-of-tune harmonies.

It was, thought Taz, the most beautiful sound she'd ever heard.

• • •

'The Missing Peace' was commissioned by the young writers of King Edwards VI Balaam Wood Academy, Birmingham: Majdi, Baha, Carter, Tayla, Roni, Alfie, Jordan, Blake, Ladja, Jubair, Sophie, Skye, Fathi, Bradley, Taylor, Courtney, Damien, Kayla, Natasha and Keira.

Teachers: Mr Josh Woods and Mrs Emma Turrell.

ABOUT THE AUTHOR

Liam Brown is the author of four novels: *Real Monsters* (2015), *Wild Life* (2016), *Broadcast* (2017) and *Skin* (2019). His work has been published internationally, translated into several languages and optioned by a major Hollywood studio. He lives in Birmingham, England, with his wife and two children.

LIAM SAYS:

I'll admit I was a tad nervous when I discovered I'd be working with a group of Year 7s at King Edwards VI Balaam Wood Academy in Frankley, Birmingham. I thought back to myself at that age: slumped at the back of the classroom in my oversized blazer and Kickers loafers, trying to avoid the teacher's gaze while I surreptitiously traded wrestling cards and POGs with my fellow students under the desk, so shy that I would barely stutter a squeak if a grown-up so much as looked in my direction…

Fortunately, it seems eleven and twelve-year-olds are significantly more mature than they were back in the mid-90s. Indeed, I was pleasantly surprised when Mrs Turrell introduced me to a group of smart, confident and unbelievably creative young people, who were quick to tell me exactly what they were looking for in a story. They wanted mystery and intrigue, with a healthy dollop of horror. They wanted abandoned buildings and haunted amusement parks. They wanted a school-age runaway as a protagonist. I could hardly keep up with them, so fast were the ideas flowing.

The real magic came when we were brainstorming possible titles for our story. Right at the beginning of our session, I made it clear that I didn't care about spelling or grammar or handwriting. It might be a funny thing for a novelist to admit, but I'm always mixing up 'there' with 'their' and 'they're'. I never know where to stick an apostrophe, and my writing looks like it was done by a drunken spider wearing ice skates. "Don't worry about any of that stuff," I said. "That's what a spell-checker is for – let's just focus on the ideas!"

Taking me at my word, one of the students suggested we call the story 'The Missing Peace'. The accidental typo was the spark I was looking for, and from that moment on, the story more or less wrote itself...

Sealed with a Loving Kiss

Lauren James

The snowman was nearly finished when Paige heard the noise. She was just sticking twig arms into the round, hard-packed snow of its belly when she became aware of a quiet popping.

She pulled out her earphones, wondering if it was just static from the podcast she was listening to. But the noise was real: a low, distant thrumming.

Paige turned around to see if it was her parents' car approaching. It was a snow day and they had both gone work, but there was a chance that they'd been sent home. The street was empty. The noise was getting louder.

Then there was a bright spark of light in the sky, getting bigger and bigger. With an ear-popping screech, the glowing light fell towards her. Paige backed away, shuffling quickly through the wet slush. The grass was slick and damp beneath the snow. As it came even nearer, the deafening noise vibrating in her eardrums, she threw herself across the lawn. It was almost on her. She squeezed her eyes shut against the blinding light, held her breath, and –

There was a dull thump, followed by a hissing sound, like water dropped on hot coals.

Paige opened her eyes. Her beautiful snowman, with its pebble eyes and carrot nose, mustard-yellow scarf and woollen hat, was gone.

She'd been working on that snowman all morning. Her mum had told her to spend her day off school looking for a work experience placement for next term, or revising for her mock GCSEs. But the snow had been too white and fresh to resist. As soon as her parents left for work, she'd put her wellies on and gone stomping out into the garden, trampling the delicate fluffy crystals into brown mush. She'd spent all morning making her snowman, listening to the *Welcome to Night Vale* podcast and eating Maoams.

Now it was just a smouldering pile of ice on the ground. The bright light had gone, and instead there was something smoking in the snow.

Paige pulled out her phone, wondering if she should call 999. What if it was a bomb? It didn't seem dangerous, though. In fact, the smouldering soon stopped completely. The whole thing had happened so quickly that none of the neighbours had even come out to investigate. Surely it wouldn't harm her, whatever it was?

Instead of phoning the police, she started recording a video. Taking a step closer, she paused, waiting to see if anything happened. She took another step, and then a third, until she was standing right over the remains of the snowman.

There was a small icy object lying there. It was jagged and dark, buried in layers of ice. It definitely wasn't a bomb – it looked more like a chunk of rock, covered in ice like a snowball.

It must be a meteorite! Paige crouched down and carefully nudged it onto the lawn. It was about the size of a book, as well as rectangular and narrow.

She poked it experimentally. She'd been expecting the meteorite to be hot, but it was cool to the touch. Too late, she wondered if she should be wearing gloves. Were meteorites toxic? What if she damaged it in some way? Or she might have contaminated it with human bacteria.

If it had really come from space, then it might be of scientific interest. How often did people find real, actual meteorites? A museum might want to buy it off her – or the newspapers might pay for pictures!

Paige quickly made a plan. She would take some photos and then move the meteorite inside, before someone else came to investigate. She could even put it in the freezer, so the space ice didn't melt away. Then she'd have time to decide what to do. She could even send the photos to NASA. They'd be able to tell her what to do with it.

She ran into the house and found an old Celebrations tin, left over from Christmas. After padding it out with clean tea towels, she lifted the meteorite into the tin with a metal spatula and carefully wrapped it up.

The freezer was full, so she emptied out a drawer for it. She could eat the frozen pizza and apple strudel for lunch – it was a snow day, after all. She had to fend for herself.

Once she'd taken some more photos of the crash site, Paige carefully kicked over the rest of the snowman. She didn't want any meteorite hunters to track her down. It belonged to her.

While the pizza cooked, Paige transferred the photos to her laptop. The meteorite didn't look anywhere near as impressive in pictures as it had in real life. It just looked like a muddy puddle of slush. It definitely didn't look dangerous, which was how it had felt at the time. She could have been badly hurt if she hadn't jumped out of the way in time. But no one would think that from the photos.

She would send them to NASA anyway, just to be on the safe side. The NASA website was full of news articles about things like the latest launch to the International Space Station, a statue to celebrate the anniversary of the first spacecraft in the 1950s, and the breakage of an old satellite. But Paige couldn't find anywhere to report a meteorite.

She did find a website called the UK Meteor Network where she could report a meteor sighting, but she would have to give the exact address she'd seen it.

She mulled this over while she ate her pizza. She was

reluctant to give out her address in case they confiscated her meteorite. Paige wanted to keep it. It was the most exciting thing that had ever happened to her, and she didn't want it to be over before it had even begun. Besides, according to the website's live feed, someone nearby had already reported seeing a shooting star. If they already knew about it she didn't need to bother, did she?

Paige decided to keep it to herself. She could always change her mind if she felt guilty about it in a few days. But she deserved this little secret, just to help her get through GCSE revision.

Mind made up, she pulled out her Maths homework and started studying.

The next morning, Paige had an email saying that school was running normally again, even though it was still snowing outside. She had a bowl of Shreddies for breakfast and watched her mum bustle around the kitchen as she got ready for work.

'Did you find a work experience placement?' her mum asked. 'And have you seen my phone charger?'

'No,' Paige said, getting the leftover apple strudel out of the fridge. They'd had it for pudding after dinner the night before, and there was still a wedge left. She could take it to school for lunch. 'I don't know where I want to go.'

Next term, her whole year group had to spend two weeks on a placement for work experience. A lot of her friends were going to the local primary school or pet rescue centre, but Paige didn't want to do that. She just couldn't decide what she did want to do. She really liked maths, but it wasn't like she could go and volunteer at a maths rescue centre.

She was putting the strudel in her lunchbox when something cold soaked into her sock. There was water leaking out of the bin.

'Ew, Mum, there's something gross on the floor,' Paige said, peeling off her damp sock.

'What?' Her mum was looking under the kitchen table for her charger. 'Oh, that – I found a bit of rubbish in the freezer, taking up all the space. Something your dad was messing around with, probably.'

Paige's heart stopped. She opened the bin, horrified. Her lovely meteorite was lying in a bed of rotten banana skins and the raw chicken juices from an empty meat packet. She'd been so careful not to contaminate the meteorite with any human bacteria, and now it was covered in goo.

'Mum!' she yelled. 'That was mine! I was saving it!'

Her mum grimaced. 'What even is it?'

'It's –' Paige paused. She still didn't want to tell anyone about it. 'It was a science experiment.'

Her mum had found her charger and was heading for the front door. 'Sorry, love. Can you fix it?'

'Sure,' Paige said glumly. 'Have a good day, or whatever.'

'Byeeee!' her mum called. 'Don't forget to lock up!'

Grimacing, Paige lifted the meteorite out of the bin. The ice had melted away, leaving only the hard rock inside. Paige ran it under the tap, wiping away a stray bit of spring onion. It wasn't rock at all, but some kind of metal. It was matt black, roughly coated in something hard and enamelled. But there were sharp, shiny steel edges, like it had been torn away from something. It looked ancient. It must have been travelling through space on an asteroid for thousands of years.

She was going to be late for school, but it was too interesting to leave. Patting it dry with a kitchen towel, she found that there were tiny indents running along one edge, as if it had been soldered. It definitely seemed to have been manufactured, rather than a natural lump of metal. It looked like a bit of computer or something. But that was impossible. It had come from space!

Paige gasped. What if it was an alien computer hard drive? Aliens could have sent this to Earth, trying to make contact with humans.

As she turned it over, something sharp poked her palm. There was a catch on the edge of the metal. It looked like there was a compartment welded onto it.

Paige grabbed the kitchen scissors and pushed the edge of the blade underneath the catch, wiggling until it popped free. It wasn't at all rusty, and it came loose with a little click. Something dark tumbled out onto the kitchen counter.

It was a tiny circle of black plastic. The disc was completely flat and covered in circular grooves, running right from the outer edge into the centre of the circle. It was perfectly intact.

It wasn't what she'd been expecting at all, but it seemed familiar somehow. She traced her finger around one of the grooves, wondering where she'd seen it before. There was a little hole in the centre, just large enough to fit her little finger in.

What was it?

Just then, the kitchen clock chimed and Paige realised that she was late for school. She pushed the disc back into the compartment and threw the meteorite into her schoolbag. She would have to run all the way there.

Paige was halfway through Biology in Period Three when she realised what the black disc was. It was a gramophone record. Those old vinyl records that people used to store music on, before they had CDs or mobiles. She remembered seeing them in old films. They were laid on a revolving table, and a needle was placed in the grooves. As the disc turned, the bumps of the needle made vibrations that were turned into sounds.

But what was an old vinyl record doing in a meteorite from outer space? They hadn't been used for decades.

When the bell rang for break, she went straight to the Music department. A teacher was there tidying up a pile of cymbals, so Paige asked, 'Excuse me, Miss? Do you know if there's a record player here anywhere?'

The teacher looked surprised. 'I think there's one in the cupboard in the hall,' she replied. 'Why?'

'I found some old records in the loft at home,' Paige said. 'Can I borrow it for a bit?'

'Of course!'

The record player was ancient, and so dusty that it clearly hadn't been used for years. But Paige managed to get it working. Nervously, she placed her record onto the turntable and lowered the needle, placing the tip into the outermost groove. Her hands were shaking.

Was she about to hear an alien message? She could be the first person ever to hear an alien voice. She started recording a video on her phone, and then let the record play.

The speakers made a crackly noise and then, out of the static, a voice said, '*Hello.*'

Paige held her breath, unable to believe it. It was a human voice!

My name is Dorothy Jackson. I'm recording this message in January 1958, in Cape Canaveral, Florida. I work at the National Aeronautics and Space Administration agency – NASA. I'm part of a team working to launch a space craft into Earth's atmosphere. We're hoping to send this 'satellite' up in just a few short months to orbit the planet.

I wanted to make a memento to accompany the spacecraft, which we're calling Vanguard 1. I work on the calculations for the orbit geometry, but I have a friend in the engineering department who's putting together a time capsule of sorts. He's going to weld it onto the inside of the satellite, and he said I could include something small if I wished. I racked my brains over what to include, and in the end I decided this voice recording would be best.

It's hard to know what to say. This message might never be heard. Or someone a thousand years from now might hear my little voice. Maybe even someone from another planet – imagine that! Hello, whoever you are. Well,

*when I think about what message I'd like to share with
the future, there's only one thing that springs to mind. I'd
like to tell you about a woman called Lily Fellowes.*

The record stopped playing then, but Paige was so
shocked it took her a moment to notice. She couldn't
believe it. She'd found a time capsule! From an ancient
satellite which had been launched in the fifties! It was
amazing that this message had survived so long. How had
it made its way to her?

Paige flipped over the record to play the other side.

*Lily works on the calculations for the Vanguard mission
as a human computer, like me. And I'm in love with her.*

At this point, Dorothy paused to take a deep breath.
Then the recording continued, in that crackly, old-fashioned American voice.

*I've never said that out loud before. I don't know what
it's like in your time, but right now when I'm from,
ladies aren't allowed to love other ladies. And, well, I
don't think that's fair. I've loved Lily since the day I met
her, and I don't ever see that changing. So, there you go
– that's my message for you.*

*I'm recording this in 1958. Lily and I can't ever be
together here, but I love her deeply and I want to leave
a record of that love, for a time when things are better
and people like us are more accepted. I hope that the
future is a little kinder than the present day. Maybe in
your time, anyone can love each other openly, like we
all deserve. That's all I have to say, I suppose. That, and*

that I hope this satellite makes it into orbit – especially after all the long hours and late nights we've all put into working on it! Thank you.

With a final crackle, the message ended.

Paige stopped her video recording, staring down at the little black disc. It was hard to believe that sixty years ago a woman had sat down and recorded that message. Her words had been orbiting the planet for all that time, just waiting for someone to hear them. And somehow they had found their way to Paige.

When she googled 'Vanguard 1', a news article came up from the day before. She realised she'd seen it on the NASA website but hadn't paid it any attention. It said:

The oldest satellite in the sky, first launched in 1958, was removed from orbit today. Retired satellites are usually directed to crash into the middle of the Pacific Ocean, the furthest point from any human habitation.

Unfortunately, when NASA attempted to guide the satellite to fall out of orbit using a controlled explosion, the satellite broke into smaller pieces. The fast-moving shrapnel crossed over Europe as it fell out of orbit, instead of falling safely into the ocean.

Multiple sightings of the falling waste – seen as shooting stars from the ground – have been recorded in France and England. Luckily, most of the pieces burnt up in the atmosphere before they could reach the ground.

> Vanguard 1 was launched in 1958 to test the use of satellites in Earth's orbit. It was the first spacecraft to use solar cells, and the transmitter remained functional until 1964. Since then, the aluminium satellite has remained in Earth's orbit, until NASA decided to remove the space debris this week in order to avoid collisions with other satellites.

Paige couldn't believe it. How had the part of the satellite, containing a long-lost message, landed safely in her garden? It felt like Dorothy had reached out a hand to her from the past, sending a message through time meant just for her.

The bell rang before she could read any more, so she hurriedly returned the record player to the cupboard, making sure the vinyl record was wrapped up safely in her bag. Now she knew how precious it was, she couldn't risk anything happening to it.

Her next lesson was ICT, so she immediately began googling Dorothy Jackson at NASA. She found an old news article about the scientist's retirement, which said that she had been a human computer who had worked on the Apollo launches during the space race. The article included a blurry monotone photograph of a black woman in a skirt suit, shaking hands with an astronaut in a NASA space suit. Apart from the article, there wasn't much information about her.

When Paige searched for Lily Fellowes, she found something even better: her Facebook page. Lily was an elderly woman now, judging by her profile picture. She was white, with grey curly hair and thick-rimmed glasses. Her information stated that she had worked in the Flight Mechanics Division at NASA for thirty-five years. It didn't look like she had ever married.

Paige wondered if Dorothy had ever told Lily how she felt. Had Lily ever known that her co-worker loved her so much that she had launched a message into space, just so that people a thousand years in the future might learn about it one day?

Suddenly, Paige knew what she had to do. She couldn't give the piece of Vanguard 1 shrapnel to a museum or science lab. She had to give it to the person it was meant for: Lily. It was hers more than anyone else's. It was too personal to become a news story or exhibition piece.

Paige sent Lily a Facebook message, attaching the video she'd recorded of Dorothy's message playing on the record player. She also sent some pictures of the snowman after the shrapnel had hit it, and the hidden compartment welded into its metal casing.

She wrote,

Hi Lily,

I don't know if you've seen the news, but yesterday the Vanguard 1 satellite fell out of Earth's orbit.
I think you worked on its launch in 1958 with your friend Dorothy Johnson. A piece of the satellite landed in my back garden in England yesterday, and there was an old vinyl record hidden inside. It was a recording made by Dorothy. I've attached a video, because I think you might like to hear it.

You don't have to reply if you don't want to, but I'm curious – are you and Dorothy still friends now? Did she ever tell you how she felt?

I really hope you were both happy. I thought her message was really lovely. She sounds like an amazing person. If you'd like, I can send you the vinyl record in the post. I think you deserve to have it.

Paige

Drawing in a deep breath, Paige sent the message. She wanted to wait and see if Lily replied, but she had already missed the start of the ICT lesson. She raced to catch up on the coding activity the rest of the class were doing, nervous butterflies fluttering in her stomach. Had she done the right thing? Would Lily be really angry when she read her message? What if it upset her?

It was too late to take it back now. All Paige could do was wait.

Paige stared at the Facebook chat box all the way home, hoping for a reply from Lily. To her amazement, the message to Lily was marked 'seen'. Lily hadn't replied yet, but this was already more than Paige had hoped for.

That whole evening and most of the next day, she could think about nothing but Lily and Dorothy. There was only a week before she had to decide on her work experience placement, but she couldn't focus on that at all.

The wait was agonising. Finally, she woke up to find a new message, from Lily. It had been sent in the early hours of the morning from America. It was a video.

Paige clicked 'play', waiting impatiently for it to buffer.

An old woman smiled into the camera, with a face full of wrinkles. Lily pushed her glasses up her nose and said, 'Is it going?'

From the background, another American voice said, 'Sure is!'

Lily said, 'Hello, Paige! Thank you so much for your message. You don't know how happy you've made me. It was like a time capsule to the happiest period of my life, hearing Dottie's voice again.

'It's such an extraordinary coincidence that you found her message like that. She kept the whole thing a complete secret – I never knew she recorded it! What a delight.

'The truth is, I loved her too. From the first day we met, she was my best friend and my favourite person. We spent every day together, computing sums and chatting away. I loved her, but I had absolutely no idea she felt the same way. I wish she'd just told me, instead of launching a message off into outer space!'

From behind the camera, that other voice said, 'Hey!'

Lily grinned. 'We worked together for years, but she moved to a different agency in the seventies. Eventually we fell out of touch. When I got your message, we hadn't spoken in decades – but I still thought about her often. She was the great lost love of my life. I've always regretted not telling her how I felt.

'So, when I heard her love letter from all those years ago, you can imagine what a shock it gave me! I had no idea if she still loved me in that way, or if she'd got married since I last knew her. But I knew I had to find her.

'Yesterday, I tracked Dottie down. It turns out she's been living in the next town over for all this time. I played her the video of her record and told her that I'd always felt the same way. And then I proposed to her.' Lily's face creased up into a radiant smile.

From behind the camera, the second voice said, 'And I said yes!'

Dorothy appeared in the frame, wrapping an arm around Lily and waving into the camera. She was in her eighties, with pure white curls and bright pink lipstick. A pair of reading glasses were hanging on a chain round her neck.

Lily kissed Dorothy on the cheek, then turned back to the camera. 'Paige, I can't tell you how much you've changed my life. I never thought I could be this happy. I'm eighty-four, but I feel like my life is just beginning! If I hadn't heard Dottie's message, I never would have reached out to her.'

Dorothy clasped Lily's hand to her chest. 'We couldn't get married then, my love. But we can now. We can make up for lost time.'

Lily gazed at Dorothy for a moment, and then said, 'Oh, one last thing! Paige, I wanted to show you this.'

She held a photograph up to the camera. It showed a pair of young women in fifties dresses, posing next to a NASA spacecraft which was preparing for launch. They had their arms around each other, grinning madly at the camera. Paige could see the same smiles on the old women holding up the photo.

'If we can ever do anything for you,' Dorothy said, 'just say the word. We owe you!'

When the footage ended, Paige found herself in tears. She couldn't believe how happy they were. It was pure chance that Dorothy and Lily had been brought back together. If Paige hadn't been making that snowman, then none of this would have happened.

Wiping her damp cheeks, Paige wrote them a long message, which she was sure was mostly incoherent with emotion. At the end, she added:

> And if you're serious about the favour, there is one thing you could do for me in return. If you still have any connections at NASA, I'm looking for a work experience placement. I'm pretty decent at Maths... and it would be nice to give you back your vinyl record in person.

• • •

'Sealed With A Loving Kiss' was commissioned by the young writers of Year 9 at Queensbridge School, Birmingham.

ABOUT THE AUTHOR

 **Lauren James** is the twice Carnegie-nominated British Young Adult author of *The Loneliest Girl in the Universe*, *The Quiet at the End of the World*, *The Reckless Afterlife of Harriet Stoker* and The Next Together series, as well as the dyslexia-friendly novellas *The Starlight Watchmaker* and *The Deep Sea Duke*, and the serialised online novel *An Unauthorised Fan Treatise*.

She has been shortlisted for the YA Book Prize, and is an Arts Council grant recipient. She teaches creative writing for Coventry University, WriteMentor, and Writing West Midlands, providing creative writing courses to children through the Spark Young Writers programme.

www.laurenejames.co.uk

LAUREN SAYS:

I had so much fun brainstorming this story with the group at Queensbridge School. I write science fiction based on real science, so we started plotting our story by reading some recent science news stories about things like Neanderthals and medieval herbal remedies.

There was one report about Ultima Thule, an asteroid shaped like a snowman, which captured everyone's imaginations. We brainstormed ways to turn the news story into a real story, and developed the idea of a meteorite crashing into a snowman on Earth, only to be discovered by a teenage girl. I was left with the fun task of deciding what happens next!

I chose to honour the computational work done by women like Katherine Johnson and Mary Jackson at NASA during the space race, an invaluable contribution to science which has been largely forgotten.

Chordae Tendineae

Ken Preston

My father's a loser.

That's the only thing you need to know about *him*.

Well, maybe there is one other thing, but we'll get to that later.

My name is Shahzana. Almost everyone calls me Shaz, except my mum. She says she called me Shahzana for a reason. She says that Shahzana means Princess, because that's what I am: her princess.

Yeah, right.

My mum's pretty cool, yeah? I mean, she's a heart surgeon, which is amazing. Unlike my father, who is a complete and utter loser. Did I mention that already?

But as cool as my mum is, she still named me wrong.

Cos I ain't no princess.

Mum brought me up on her own. That's because my father, The Loser, left us when I was only six months old. Just disappeared.

Mum says she was scared out of her mind at the time. She thought he'd been murdered or had an accident or something. But then he took all the money out of our account (not that we had much) and Mum had to close it and open up a new one. And the police never found a body or anything – it was like he'd walked out of the house and decided not to come back.

Wait a minute, I'm telling this story all wrong. But sometimes it's difficult to know where to start.

Maybe I should start with Grandma, and the burglars breaking into her house and attacking her.

She's The Loser's mother but, unlike her son, she's pretty ace. After The Loser left Mum, Grandma looked after us both. She looked after me while Mum continued her studies at medical school, and when Mum started working.

She's still looking after us now.

But wait, Grandma didn't get burgled! That turned out to be a lie.

And now I'm telling the story all backwards.

So I'm going to start with the first time I met Lenore.

It happened the day after the break-in, when I took the bus to the hospital to visit Grandma after school. They'd kept her in overnight for observation, as she'd been beat up and banged her head. Mum had already seen her the night before in the Emergency Department.

By the time I arrived, big fat drops of rain were falling from the sky. I just managed to run from the bus stop and into the hospital before the heavens really opened up. Inside the entrance, I turned and watched the rain. It was a deluge, like a wall of water.

Grandma was on Ward B6, in a bay with three other beds. The curtains had been pulled around Grandma's bed and I could hear a low murmur of voices. That meant a doctor or a nurse was in there with her. I didn't want to disturb them, so I stood outside the curtains and waited.

'Get out of here!' Grandma hissed suddenly. I had never heard such venom in her voice before.

The curtain whipped back in front of me, and I found myself face to face with Lenore. She was tall and looked down at me like I was something unpleasant and stinky she had found on the bottom of her shoe.

Lenore was tall and elegant and beautiful. She had heart-shaped eyes and blood-red lips, and she was as pale as death. I didn't know Lenore's name then – I only found that out later.

I should have stepped out of her way as fast as I could move. I wanted to. But I couldn't. Those eyes of hers held me, trapped me where I stood. Like an exotic butterfly pinned on a board and examined through a magnifying glass.

Lenore's blood-red lips curled in disgust.

'Beti,' Grandma said, reaching out her hands and beckoning me over.

The movement and Grandma's voice broke the spell,

and I stepped to one side. Still, Lenore did not make a move to leave. Her head simply rotated on her long, slender neck, her eyes following me as I backed away.

'Yeh larki churail hai!' Grandma hissed.

I grabbed her wrinkled, bony hand, and it gripped mine tight. Her palm was warm in mine.

Lenore turned and walked away, gliding from the ward as though she were carried by invisible currents of air.

'Who is she, Grandma?' I whispered.

'Churail,' Grandma said, her eyes still locked on Lenore's retreating form.

Then she pulled me close and hugged me.

'I don't understand,' I said.

Grandma chuckled. 'You think you should understand everything? You think you are so grown up now, but you are still a child. You do not need to know everything. Not yet, at least.'

'But that woman, is she going to hurt you?'

Grandma shook her head and held me even tighter. 'No, she cannot hurt me.'

There's something you need to know about my grandmother. She's not your typical old lady who sits at home and spies on the neighbours. She's strong-willed and independent, and that's how she's always been. And if she was telling me that Lenore couldn't hurt her, then I believed it.

No one messed with Grandma.

Up until now I had been captivated with Lenore, but now she had gone I noticed the bruising and scratches on

Grandma's face. One eye was puffed shut and her neck was covered in yellow bruises.

'Grandma!'

She waved her hand at me. 'Shush, it's nothing.'

'But the police, have they –?'

Grandma muttered something in Hindi.

'Stop, Grandma, you know I can't understand when you speak Hindi.'

She gave me that look, the one reserved for when she is feeling particularly disappointed and let down. 'Your mother told me you were learning.'

'I tried, but it's too difficult.' I tore my eyes from hers and looked at the floor. It seemed the safest thing to do.

I heard Grandma huff. 'Too difficult. You should spend less time on that machine of yours, doing whatever it is you do.'

'It's an iPhone, Grandma.'

'Well, I never see you making any phone calls on it.'

I looked up again and Grandma was smiling at me, the laughter lines around her eyes crinkled up. Even through the bruising and swelling, Grandma's spirit shone bright and strong.

'How are you feeling today?' I said.

'Much better. The doctor thinks I can go home tomorrow.'

That was great news. I'd been really worried about her.

We chatted some more until she grew tired and I decided I should leave.

Grandma wanted me to call Mum and ask her to come

and collect me. But Mum was working and, besides, I was old enough that I didn't need collecting.

I kissed Grandma goodbye on her cheek, being careful not to hurt her. When I pulled back, Grandma held on tight to my hand and gave me a fierce, almost frightening look.

'You go straight home!' she hissed. 'Go home and lock the doors and don't let anyone in.'

'Except Mum, yeah?' I said.

Her eyes softened a little, and she smiled. 'Yes, except for Mum.'

Back down at the hospital's entrance, I stood just inside the automatic doors and watched the rain hitting the cars and the ambulances pulling up outside. How could there be so much water in the sky? And it was dark out there, like middle-of-the-night dark.

I flinched at the touch of a hand on my shoulder and, when I turned around, I flinched again.

Lenore.

That look of disgust had gone, but her beautiful face still unsettled me. What was it about her that did that? Those lips, maybe? A little too full and red. Or her eyes? Her pupils were wide and dark.

'I think this rain will not stop for a while,' she said.

I tore my eyes from her and looked at the rain again. 'Why were you and Grandma arguing?' Her hand was still on my shoulder. She was gentle, but I had to resist the urge to shake her off. I had a feeling that might not be a good idea, although I didn't know why.

'I have a car,' Lenore said. 'Let me drive you home and we can talk about that.'

Yeah right, like that was going to happen. I stepped away, and her hand slid off my shoulder.

'Are you serious?' I said. 'I'm not getting in a car with you! How stupid do you think I am?'

Lenore's red lips parted in a tiny smile. She turned and strode out of the hospital and – I swear to you now, I'm telling you the truth – it looked like she walked right through that downpour and not one drop of rain landed on her.

Not one.

A car pulled up and Lenore opened the passenger door and climbed inside. The windows were tinted black and I couldn't see anything inside.

I walked down to the hospital canteen and got myself a Coke and sat down at a table. I thought maybe Grandma was right after all and I should call Mum. Wait for her to come and pick me up. The rain wasn't the only reason I didn't want to go outside tonight.

As usual, my call went straight to voicemail, but I knew Mum would pick it up as soon as she could. I sat and swigged the Coke straight from the bottle. Mum was always telling me off for that. She said that when the bottles were being transported rats peed all over them. She said that when I drank straight from the bottle I was basically drinking Coke-flavoured rat pee.

Mum'll tell me all sorts of rubbish sometimes.

That got me thinking about Grandma again. She wasn't

like that. She either spoke her mind and told it to you straight, or she said it was none of your business and clammed up. That's what she was doing now. Whoever Lenore was, and whatever the business between them, Grandma wasn't saying.

I thought about going back up to the ward and asking her again, but I checked the time on my phone and realised the ward was closed to visitors.

In the end I decided I was being pathetic and I should just go home. It looked like the rain had stopped, anyway.

Back home, the house was quiet and empty.

I lay on my bed and watched TV for a while, and eventually I dozed off.

A light tapping at my door jerked me awake.

'Shahzana, can I come in?'

I pushed myself up to a sitting position. My head was groggy and still full of sleep. 'Yeah.'

Mum came in and sat down at the end of my bed. 'How's Grandma?'

'She's fine, she says she's coming home tomorrow.'

Mum smiled. 'That's good. I'll collect her, and she can stay here. I don't want her going home just yet.'

'She had this woman visiting her. Grandma didn't like her. I don't know who she is and Grandma won't say.'

Mum frowned. 'Your grandma can be a very mysterious woman sometimes. She drives me mad.'

'Yeah, me too.' I paused for a moment, trying to recall something Grandma had said to me. 'Mum, what does churail mean?'

Mum's frown deepened. 'Who said that word to you? Grandma?'

I nodded.

'A churail is a devil, a supernatural being that sucks the life out of you. They're a myth, a story to frighten little children with.'

'Why would Grandma be talking about devils and monsters?'

Mum shook her head. 'Who knows? We'll ask her when she comes home, ok?' Mum paused, giving me one of her looks. Not one of her You are in so much trouble looks. No, this was one of her thoughtful, pondering looks.

'What?' I said.

'How was your day?'

'All right. School, you know.'

Mum sighed.

I held up a hand before she could speak. 'I know, I know, I need to work hard and get good grades on my exams, and this is the only time in my life when education is free, and I should enjoy learning, and –'

'And blah, blah, blah!' Mum said and shoved me playfully. 'Do I really nag you that much?'

I put on a mock, thoughtful look. 'Hmm, let me think…'

Mum held her hands up in surrender. 'All right, all right, I know.'

'How was your day?' I said.

Mum nodded. 'Good. I had a case today repairing the chordae tendineae in an old man's heart.'

I scooped a hand over my head. 'Whoa, hold on, I'm

already out of my depth. What are chord… tendee…'

'Chordae tendineae. They're tough strands, like string, which hold certain valves shut in the heart to prevent a backflow of blood in the heart's chambers.'

'Oookaaaaayyyy,' I said. 'So, they're like strings in your heart, holding things together.'

Mum smiled. 'Heart strings. Yes, exactly.' Mum reached out and tousled my hair like I was five again. 'And you, you tug on my heart strings all the time, especially when I have to be at work so often, and so late.'

I pushed her hand away. 'Mum! I'm not a little kid anymore, and I've told you I'm fine.'

'I know you're fine,' Mum said, and smiled sadly. 'Have you eaten yet?'

I shook my head.

'Me neither. How about we order pizza?'

I grinned. 'Do you seriously need an answer? Yes!'

So, even though it was a school night, we had pizza and we watched a silly film on Netflix, and Mum drank wine and I drank Coke-flavoured rat pee.

And we had the best time ever.

When I finally went to bed, my head was buzzing and I couldn't get to sleep. What was I thinking about: churail and blood sucking creatures? The mysterious Lenore? Grandma?

No, I was thinking about The Loser and about how much I hated him. If he hadn't abandoned us, then I would have had someone at home when Mum was working, and she wouldn't have had to worry about working so hard.

47

How different would our lives have been if The Loser had never left?

But then, considering what he did, maybe it was for the best that he wasn't around. Maybe we were better off without him.

Eventually I fell asleep.

I can't remember what time it was when I woke up. It was the middle of the night, though. Possibly the deepest, darkest part of the night, maybe when churail wandered the streets, looking for victims.

I jerked awake just like I had when Mum had knocked before. But when I looked at my bedroom door, it was closed. Then I heard it again.

A light tap-tap-tapping on my bedroom window.

I sat up and pulled the duvet up under my chin.

… tap… tap… tap…

I shivered, and goosebumps sprang up on my arms and neck.

… tap… tap… tap…

What was it? Something flapping in the wind, like the end of a branch, perhaps. Except we didn't have any trees that close to the house. Maybe a bird? Or… something else?

… tap… tap… tap…

Curiosity battled with my fear until my fear gave in and retreated. But only a little.

I climbed out of bed, my hands still gripping the duvet.

… tap… tap… tap…

I let go of the duvet and padded barefoot across the

hard, wooden floor. The soles of my feet tingled from th
cold. I stopped in front of the drawn curtains, but I made
no move to pull them back.

Shahzana…

I flinched like I'd been slapped in the face. Where had
that come from? Was the voice real or just in my head?

… tap… tap… tap… Shahzana…

I saw my hands, possessed of a will of their own, reach
out and grip the curtain fabric, bunching the edges up in
my fists. I yanked the curtains apart.

I saw Lenore floating outside my bedroom window. She
tapped at the windowpane with her long, scarlet fingernails. Her face and hands were impossibly white, her eyes
dark like pools of deep water, and her hair was lustrous
and shiny, framing her beautiful face. But her full, red lips
were obnoxiously, repellently disgusting.

Shahzana… Let me in…

… tap… tap… tap…

She smiled, and I saw her sharp, pointed fangs. She bit
down on her bottom lip and a round blob of bright blood
bubbled from the wound and ran down her chin.

My head throbbed as I looked at her, like she was inside
and pounding on my skull. But no matter how much I
wanted to tear my eyes off her, to throw my arms over my
face and stumble away, I couldn't. Once more, with a will
of their own, my hands crept towards the window.

… Let me in… Shahzana…

I pulled the handle up and swung my window open.
Shahzana hovered there, as a cool night breeze caressed
my face. I thought she would lunge through the window

was a vampire.

... Shahzana... Can I come in..?

I shook my head, the movement jerky as though I was a puppet being operated by strings.

Lenore opened her mouth, revealing those pearly white teeth. Scarlet blood still trickled down her chin. Her long, pointed tongue flicked out and licked her lips.

... Let me in, Shahzana...

Her eyes, so deep and black, like pools of water I could fall into, held me in place.

I had no choice. I had to invite her in.

I opened my mouth to speak the words.

'You can –'

An ambulance's siren cut through the night, the sound sudden and shocking. Lenore broke eye contact with me as she whipped her head around, distracted by the noise.

Released from her hold, I slammed the window shut and drew the curtains. I ran to my bed and pulled up the duvet, over my head and everything.

Stupid, I know. Like that was going to protect me.

But I knew that Lenore couldn't come inside the house unless I invited her in.

And no way was I going to do that.

The following morning, my encounter with Lenore seemed like a dream. Over breakfast Mum asked me if I was all right and I just said I was tired. What was the point in telling her? She would just tell me I had a nightmare.

And I was starting to think maybe that was all it was.

A stupid dream.

I left the house and headed for school. The sun was shining, and that felt good after my dream last night.

But then I saw the car. The one that had picked Lenore up at the hospital. The one with windows tinted black.

Was that to protect Lenore from the sunlight? Was the driver a vampire too?

All day I couldn't get Lenore out of my head. I can't remember a single lesson I had at school, or anything my mates said. I must have looked like a sleepwalker.

When I got home that afternoon, Mum was home and so was Grandma, sitting in her favourite armchair.

I ran over and gave her a massive hug.

'I'm not complaining, but what's this for?' she said, chuckling.

Fair question. I'm not usually known for my extravagant displays of affection.

'I'm just glad you're here.' I sat down cross-legged on the carpet. 'Now we can look after you for a while.'

Grandma smiled. 'A little while. And then I will go home.'

'Do you have to? You could come and live with us all the time.'

Grandma just smiled and gave me a look. It was the same one my mum had given me last night. Weird, seeing as how they're not related.

When it was time to go to bed, I thought of Lenore again, floating at my window, tapping her red fingernails against

…i asking to be let inside. It seemed more like than ever, but that didn't stop the goosebumps ..o on my arms.

What's wrong?' Grandma said.

I pulled my sleeves down. 'Nothing. Goodnight.'

My room was cold, so I changed quickly and climbed under the duvet. I pulled it up under my chin and looked at the curtains pulled across the window.

Why hadn't I told Mum, or Grandma?

Because they would have laughed at me?

Because I didn't believe it myself?

I lay awake for ages, listening to the creaks of the house settling. An owl hooted outside.

I closed my eyes, trying to think of nice things, trying to count backwards from a hundred. Nothing worked. I just couldn't get to sleep.

… tap… tap… tap…

I snapped my eyes open.

I hadn't been dreaming.

And Lenore was back.

… tap… tap… tap…

All I had to do was stay right where I was in my warm, comfortable bed and ignore her. Lenore couldn't come in without me inviting her.

… tap… tap… tap…

And I wasn't about to do that.

… tap… tap… tap…

Was I?

… Let me in, Shahzana…

I clapped my hands over my ears and screwed my eyes shut.

Go away! I thought. *Go away and leave me alone!*

No way was I leaving this bed. No way. Absolutely no –

I pulled back the curtains, and there was Lenore.

How had this happened?

Lenore smiled at me through the windowpane. She scratched at the glass with her long, scarlet fingernails.

… Let me in, Shahzana…

I pulled up the handle and pushed the window open. It was like listening to someone else speak. I heard my voice form words:

'Come in,' it said. 'You can come in now.'

Lenore floated in through the open window. Her hands clasped my cheeks, and her flesh was so very cold.

I couldn't move. I couldn't speak or scream for help.

With her thumb, Lenore wiped away a tear running down my cheek.

'Don't cry,' she whispered. 'It only hurts a little and then you will be free.'

Her breath was freezing cold and stank of moist earth and rotting flesh. As she pushed my head back, exposing my throat, she opened her mouth wide. It looked like an empty grave. Then she froze, her head tipped back, and she screamed.

I pulled myself free and stumbled to the end of my bed.

Lenore had a wooden stake protruding from her chest, blood dripping from its sharpened point. She sank to her knees, revealing Grandma standing behind her, another stake raised and ready to plunge.

'That is how you deal with churail,' she said.

Lenore's face trembled. She arched her head back as her features twisted and writhed. Her flesh bubbled and popped, and yellow pus ran from the open sores. Those once full, red lips shrivelled up and peeled back as her teeth turned rotten and dropped from her mouth.

Finally she fell forwards onto the carpet. Her body continued to writhe beneath her clothes. Her fingers curled into clawed bones and dropped from her hands. Her lustrous hair turned grey and fell out of her skull. Her body continued disintegrating until finally there was nothing left but her clothes and a pile of ash.

A sob from the window startled us.

Crouched in the open window was a man. The wind tugged at his shirt and his long hair. I didn't need to see the blood on his lips or those piercing eyes to know that he was a vampire too.

'Leave!' Grandma spat the word out like it was poison and lifted the stake in her hand. 'Leave now or I will kill you!'

The vampire didn't move. He didn't even look at Grandma. He just stared at me.

And I knew. Don't ask me how, because I can't explain that, but I knew that it was The Loser.

He turned and jumped from the window. I ran over and leaned out, but he was nowhere to be seen.

'Dad?'

Dad?

Later that morning, when the sun had come up and the events of last night could have been a dream but for the human-shaped pile of ash on my bedroom floor, Grandma told us everything. How all those years ago The Loser had got himself mixed up with some bad types, how he became a vampire, and how Grandma forbade him from ever seeing his family again.

Or she would kill him. So he left the country. Grandma never saw him again.

Until a couple of days ago, when he turned up at Grandma's house with Lenore. Said he wanted his family back.

'He wanted you, Raajakumaaree,' Grandma said. 'He wanted you to become a vampire and join him, but he didn't have the guts to do it himself, which is why he came to see me first.'

Grandma told him no. Told him to leave again, or she would kill them both.

Nobody had broken into Grandma's house. Lenore had attacked Grandma.

The Loser had pulled Lenore off and fled into the night with her.

'Do you think he still loves me?' I said, and then felt stupid for even considering it, let alone saying it. Was I so pathetic that I needed The Loser's love?

Grandma, as if sensing how I felt, placed a hand on mine. 'I think he does.'

'Heart strings,' Mum took my other hand. 'You have been tugging on his heart strings.'

I thought of him crouched in the open window. He hadn't looked at Lenore – he'd looked at me. And maybe, just maybe, that had been love I saw in his eyes.

He's still a loser, though.

Not like my mum. She's ace.

And my vampire-slaying Grandma?

She's the best.

• • •

'Chordae Tendineae' was commissioned by the young writers of Ark Boulton Academy, Birmingham: Areeba, Zara, Rayeema, Raiden, Tayyab, Momina, Mariyar, Haris, Adil, Hajrah, Muhammed, Hamza, Ezan, Aisha and Ayub.

Teacher: Miss Jessica Lee.

ABOUT THE AUTHOR

 Brain surgeon, former Mr Universe, rock star, world champion surfer, secret agent, eloquent in twelve languages, and special adviser to the world's leaders, **Ken Preston** loves telling lies for a living.

KEN SAYS:

This commission presented a unique opportunity for me to step out of my comfort zone: I had to write a short story based around the ideas provided by a group of secondary school pupils, and a theme provided by the Read On facilitators.

Reflecting upon my visit with the brilliant pupils at Ark Boulton Academy, all of them from minority ethnic backgrounds, I realised I would be failing them if I placed the usual British white child at the centre of the story. But then of course I worried about committing an act of cultural appropriation.

Another challenge was the clash between the theme of the anthology, Love, and the pupils' desire that the story should feature vampires.

Fortunately, I was able to call on the guidance of a friend of mine whose grandmother had lived in Haryana in

North India. She provided the translation from English to Hindi (which proved very helpful, as Google Translate thinks "Yeh larki churail hai!" in English is "This girl is a chicken!") and my friend Pardip Basra gave me some cultural references to vampires in Indian Muslim folklore. Pardip also read the final draft and gave it his approval. Thank you, Pardip.

I enjoyed writing this story so much, and I fell in love with Shahzana and her mother and grandmother.

Also, wouldn't you just love to have a vampire-slaying grandma?

The Boy & The Cricket

Bali Rai

The Magic Bird shook its head. Purple feathers tipped in gold, sapphire eyes and a sharp crimson beak marked it as unusual. It was.

'Only one way out,' it said.

'And that is..?'

'You must right your last wrong,' the Magic Bird replied.

'My last wrong?'

'I don't like repeating myself,' said the Magic Bird. 'Now go, before I decide to eat you after all.'

'But how do I proceed?'

'That's your problem,' the Magic Bird replied. 'You have one week from sunrise tomorrow. The Prophecy should be a clue...'

Arjun grew dismayed. The Bhags had trampled dirt across the freshly-washed stone floor.

'Clean it again,' said Mr Bhag, a corpulent and cruel man.

The childless Bhags were Arjun's guardians. Wealthy merchants who had rescued him from the filthy streets of the teeming city.

'But I've only just finished washing it,' Arjun complained.

'Now, now,' said Mrs Bhag, wagging a stumpy index finger. 'Do not complain. Be thankful that we were kind enough to rescue you.'

'But I…'

'Enough!' she spat. 'Show some gratitude, disgusting creature!'

She picked up a pot of cold stew.

'Oh dear,' she said to her husband. 'I seem to have made a mess.'

The earthen pot smashed against ochre flagstones. Unctuous brown chicken casserole pooled.

'And when you're done,' she said to Arjun, 'you can make more.'

Arjun held his tongue. Ruined stew was a small price to pay. The scars on his legs and torso spoke of far more painful punishments. He was enslaved, and at the Bhags' mercy.

'You have a bed and food to eat,' Mr Bhag told him. 'When we found you, you were half naked and starving. Do not forget our kindness, rat.'

As they left, Arjun blinked away tears. They *had* taken him from the streets. They *had* given him a place to sleep, clothes and meagre rations. Yet he was also their slave. Scolded and insulted daily, beaten often. His existence was pitiful. He repeatedly wondered whether the streets might be the better option. He'd be hungry and dirty, but he'd also be free.

'They know nothing,' he whispered. 'I was meant for more than this!'

Arjun did not know his real name. He knew neither his true age nor his birth family's identity. Attempts at recalling his early years remained foggy.

'You were doubtless beaten as a child,' Mrs Bhag once told him. 'Struck about the head, so as to lose all memory. Explains your stupidity.'

'Who can blame his parents?' Mr Bhag added. 'Imagine this useless rat for a son. Dumped him through shame and despair, I'd wager. They have no morals about such things.'

'Probably one of several,' Mrs Bhag said. 'These peasants multiply like summer flies.'

Yet Arjun felt something else. A sense of dignity that belied his wretched existence. He would stir every night, convinced that his dreams were real. Dreams of lavish feasts and splendid surroundings. A life far removed from this.

'Perhaps I am the long-lost son of rich parents?' he would whisper to the gloom. 'They must miss me terribly and yearn for my homecoming.'

As the Bhags made life ever more difficult, Arjun's imagination created ever grander visions.

'I was a prince,' he'd say. 'A great warrior. A man of medicine, curing illness and disease.'

However, harsh reality always clawed back. A ravenous beast, eager to refute Arjun's foolish and fanciful imaginings.

Arjun swept the floors late one evening, impatient for his straw bed. A cricket settled on the windowsill. Larger than average, with a green shell and bright orange head, it watched the sullen and miserable boy work. He shuffled about without purpose. Too wretched to notice the Cricket's presence.

'Perfect,' the Cricket whispered, eyeing a pile of chicken bones.

It crept slowly around the grey stone walls. The discarded chicken reeked. So too the vegetable peelings and mouldy mango that lay beside it. The Cricket would feast well, if the boy didn't see it. Thankfully for the Cricket, chirping was not an issue. It was the only silent cricket in existence.

'A useful talent,' it said, drawing nearer to its goal.

As Arjun finished his chores, the Cricket gorged. Soon the boy lay down, fully clothed and exhausted. The Cricket ate until it grew sated. Eventually it settled in the straw, by the boy's head.

'This would make a lovely home,' the Cricket said, settling down. 'If I was planning on remaining a cricket, that is...'

Arjun's eyes immediately opened.

'Who was that?' he said aloud, eyeing the Cricket.

The insect froze, wary of being crushed.

'Just my luck,' said Arjun. 'Hearing voices. As if I don't have enough troubles.'

He considered flicking the Cricket away but changed his mind.

'Live and let live,' he said. 'Just don't start chirping and keep me awake.'

'I don't chirp,' the Cricket replied.

Arjun leapt from the bed.

'D-D-D..?' he began.

'Yes,' the Cricket said. 'I did speak…'

'But you're a…'

'Cricket, yes,' said the insect.

Arjun shook his head.

'I'm losing my mind,' he said. 'I must be losing my…'

'No, no,' said the Cricket. 'I mean I understand why you might think so. After all, whoever heard of talking insects?'

Calming a little, Arjun sat down.

'So, you're real?'

The Cricket nodded.

'Yes,' it said. 'Unless I'm very deluded.'

'Do you have a name?'

'Not that I know of,' lied the Cricket.

'Well, my name isn't even my own,' sad Arjun.

'Really?' the Cricket replied. 'Do tell…'

Arjun and the insect spoke until dawn. The boy told the Cricket everything. From his foggy memory and day-dreams of grandeur, to being found by the Bhags. The Cricket listened, saying little in return. Eventually, the boy passed out from exhaustion. He slept for an hour when Mrs Bhag burst into the kitchen.

'Wake up, you wretched beast!' she growled. 'Where is our breakfast?'

Arjun leapt from his bed, babbling excuses. Mrs Bhag ignored them. She rapped Arjun about the ribs with a rolling pin. As he howled, she hit him again.

'Useless turd!' she yelled. 'Now get up!'

The Cricket saw everything. Later, after the Bhags went out, it settled within Arjun's eye line.

'They are very cruel,' it said.

Arjun blinked twice.

'Ah,' he said. 'So, it really wasn't a dream.'

'No,' replied the Cricket. 'Now, how do we stop these wicked people?'

'What can we do?' said Arjun. 'What choice do I have?'

'My friend,' said the Cricket, 'there is always a choice.'

Later, as Arjun plodded to the bazaar district, the Cricket rested on his shoulder. The market was loud and busy, and equal parts foul and fragrant. At a fruit stall, locals gossiped about the Empress, as the poor sat by open sewers and begged for a pittance.

'They say she's a witch,' said one man.

'Aye,' said another. 'I've heard tales of black magic and sorcery.'

'Killed her own brother,' said the first. 'Although he was a vile ruler.'

The other man smiled.

'We had a party when he died.'

'Who didn't?' said the first. 'The sister's just as bad. Sooner she's gone, the better.'

'The Prophecy will come true,' said the other.

'Hail the coming of the Prophecy...' said the first.

Arjun was intrigued by the gossip.

'What is this Prophecy?'

'Oh, just superstitious nonsense,' said the Cricket. 'These people will believe anything.'

'They obviously hated the Emperor.'

'The Emperor was a nasty and wicked man,' the Cricket told him.

'How do you know?'

'I wasn't always an insect,' replied the Cricket.

'You were reincarnated and remember your past life?'

'Yes,' said the Cricket. 'It's a curse, trust me.'

'What did you do?' Arjun asked. 'To have such bad karma?'

'It's not that bad,' the Cricket protested.

Only that was also a fib.

The Cricket spent four days urging Arjun to run away. Four days during which the boy was insulted, beaten and ridiculed. On the fourth day, Mrs Bhag took umbrage at her lukewarm tea. She took a belt and proceeded to whip Arjun mercilessly. The boy's screams seemed to spur her on. Finally, as the fifth day dawned, the battered and bruised boy relented.

'I think you're right,' he told the Cricket.

'I am,' the Cricket replied. 'Stay and they will eventually kill you.'

'But where can I go?'

'Leave that to me,' said the Cricket. 'I will explain all.'

'So, explain,' said Arjun.

'Later,' the Cricket told him. 'First pack what you need. We must leave before the Bhags wake up.'

Arjun wore his only clothes and one pair of shoes. There was nothing else. Instead, he packed flatbread, fruit and chicken into a satchel, alongside the sharpest knife.

'Just in case,' he told the Cricket.

'Very wise,' the Cricket replied.

They crept into dawn, careful to remain in the shadows. A maze of narrow lanes and alleys criss-crossed the city. The Cricket seemed to know them all. Soon they were far from the Bhags' residence, approaching the Royal Palace.

'Why are we here?' Arjun asked.

'I used to work here,' the Cricket revealed. 'I know of a place we can hide.'

The fortified palace had only two heavily guarded entrances. To the north wall was a lake. The Cricket led Arjun towards it.

'There's a storm drain,' the Cricket told him. 'And a tunnel. It leads to an abandoned annexe. I'm the only one who knows it exists. The other person is dead.'

'Who was that?'

'The Emperor,' replied the Cricket.

'You knew the Emperor?'

Arjun was astonished.

'We were best friends,' said the Cricket.

The insect waited a beat,

'I *killed* him.'

They entered the storm drain and Arjun crawled through the tunnel. The Cricket nestled in the boy's hair. The secret annexe was close. Once inside, the Cricket explained all.

'My name was Deven,' it said. 'I was an assassin. The best there was. The Emperor and I were childhood friends.'

'But how could you murder your own friend?'

The Cricket paused a while, gathering thoughts.

'The Emperor grew power crazed,' it eventually replied. 'The people grew to hate his brutal ways. His sister begged me to get rid of him.'

'But why agree?' asked Arjun. 'He may have been evil, but he was your friend.'

'It's complicated,' the Cricket replied.

'Complicated?'

'You're only a boy,' said the Cricket. 'Affairs of the heart are beyond your understanding.'

'You loved the Empress?' said Arjun, proving the insect wrong.

'He wasn't supposed to die,' said the Cricket. 'The poison was to incapacitate him. Then she would depose him and take over.'

'But he died?'

'Yes,' said the Cricket. 'And she betrayed me. She used the same poison to kill me, too. Fed me infected dates. I don't even *like* dates...'

'Karma,' said Arjun.

The Cricket scowled. Or the insect equivalent, at least.

'Something like that,' it said.

Arjun eyed the slimy stone walls and tried to ignore the giant golden lizard sitting nearby. It watched them with scarlet eyes, black tongue flicking.

'So, why are we here?' asked the boy.

'I need your help,' said the Cricket. 'I need to repay Karma and win back my life.'

'I don't understand,' said Arjun.

'Don't worry,' said the Cricket, 'You will.'

The annexe was unreachable from within the palace. Unless you knew it existed. Hidden behind a false wall, with a secret stone switch for the entrance, it was a clandestine retreat.

'The Emperor's father created it,' said the Cricket. 'To hide from his sixteen wives and thirty-seven children...'

Arjun seemed shocked.

'They were different times,' said the Cricket. 'We should not judge.'

'You murdered people for a living,' Arjun reminded the Cricket. 'That's a form of judgement, is it not?'

'You're very bright,' said the Cricket. 'And very annoying.'

'Yes,' Arjun replied. 'I may be young but I'm not an idiot.'

The Cricket directed Arjun up worn steps, to the secret door.

'Push this stone,' it said, settling on the wall. 'It takes some force.'

Arjun waited for the Cricket to move and pushed. When nothing happened, he tried again.

'Harder!' the Cricket urged.

After several attempts, the mechanism finally creaked, and the door swung open. Beyond lay a vast, opulent and empty room.

'The Emperor's chambers,' said the Cricket. 'No longer used since…'

'You murdered your best friend for his sister's love.'

The Cricket would have slapped the boy. If it could have.

'Sarcasm is…'

'Entirely appropriate,' said the boy. 'Given the circumstances.'

'Be quiet and let me think,' said the Cricket. 'Time is against us.'

'What do you mean?'

The Cricket settled on a dusty windowsill. The glass was thick with grime.

'Wipe the dirt away,' said the Cricket.

'Why?'

'To see out of the window, of course!'

Arjun created a small circle with an index finger.

'Now look down at the courtyard,' said the Cricket.

The palace grounds were thick with activity. Make-shift stalls sold drinks and fruit and sweets. Several goats roasted on spits over glowing charcoal. The walls had been hung with silken drapes in scarlet and gold. A group of musicians practiced on a temporary stage. And courtiers ran around shouting orders and panicking.

'Some sort of celebration.'

'The Empress's Birthday,' said the Cricket.

'Today?'

'No, I was just making it up,' the insect replied. 'Of course, today!'

Arjun felt like slapping the insect into a pulp. He resisted. Instead he noted that gallows had also been erected.

'Why the hangman?' he asked, watching a giant man testing the ropes.

'The Empress enjoys watching executions,' the Cricket explained. 'She's putting on a show for the people.'

'Hangings?' Arjun replied. 'That's barbaric.'

'The Emperor was the same,' said the insect. 'Family tradition. Drink, eat, celebrate, kill a few people you don't like the look of.'

'Some family,' said Arjun. 'I wouldn't want to be one of them.'

'Who would?' the Cricket replied.

'None of that explains why we're here,' said Arjun.

'That's easy,' said the Cricket. 'We're going to kill the Empress so I can get my old life back.'

Arjun went over to the enormous bed and lay down.

Closing his eyes, he imagined a life of wealth and pleasure. Servants at his beck and call, a mighty palace and kingdom of his own. Making all the rules. It would be heaven.

'So?' asked the Cricket.

'No,' Arjun replied from amongst a dozen ivory pillows filled with the finest goose down. 'Can't we just stay here?'

'And do what?' asked the Cricket. 'Live in hiding, sneak out to steal food?'

'Why not?'

'Because we'd get caught and killed,' the Cricket replied. 'Well, you would. I'd just fly away. They'd probably boil you in hot water. Maybe have you trampled by elephants. Your problem…'

'So why do you need me?'

The Cricket longed for its old human form. Just so it might kick the boy.

'Because I am a cricket,' it said. 'I can't kill the Empress. You'll have to do that.'

'No!' Arjun replied. 'I'm not killing anyone. It's immoral and cruel and…'

'She's a monster!' said the Cricket. 'You'd be doing the people a favour.'

'You mean I'd be doing you a favour,' said Arjun. 'Why should I?'

'Because you would benefit too,' said the Cricket.

'Why?'

The boy closed his eyes and dreamt.

'Because I killed you!' the Cricket finally revealed.

Arjun sat up at once.

'Huh?' he said, dumbfounded.

'I killed you,' the insect repeated.

'But we've never met,' said the boy.

'Yes, we have,' said the Cricket.

'I don't…' began Arjun.

'*You* were the Emperor!'

Arjun's shock was still apparent twenty minutes later. He sat perfectly still on the Emperor's bed – *his* bed…

'All those dreams I had,' he whispered. 'All of those feelings of being more than I was.'

'Flashbacks to your previous life,' said the Cricket.

'But that doesn't happen,' said Arjun. 'People don't walk around reminiscing about their previous lives, do they?'

'A glitch in Karma, perhaps?' said the Cricket.

'I feel unattached from the Universe,' Arjun replied. 'Neither here nor there. Lost in some void.'

'There is no void,' said the Cricket. 'I wronged you and I will rectify that. You will become Emperor again…'

'All to save your own skin?'

The Cricket considered that for a moment.

'That's a happy by-product, yes,' it eventually said.

'It's your only reason,' Arjun replied.

'I was mistaken,' said the Cricket. 'I want to put that right.'

'How can you?' asked Arjun.

'Trust me,' said the Cricket.

'Trust you?' replied Arjun. 'A lying, duplicitous assassin?'

'And you were a vain and murderous ruler,' said the Cricket. 'Drunk with power and hated by the people.'

'I was that bad?'

'Yes,' said the Cricket. 'So maybe I shouldn't trust you either?'

'Fine,' said Arjun. 'I won't help you.'

'Ok,' said the Cricket. 'I'll take you back, then. I'm sure the Bhags miss you.'

Arjun considered his opulent surroundings and all the trappings of his previous existence. Compared those things with his current life. Recalled the insults, bullying and violence of his employers.

'Tell me your plan,' he said after a while. 'Maybe I will help…'

The staff and guards were too busy preparing for the festivities to notice Arjun. With the Cricket directing from his hair, the former Emperor found the kitchens with ease. The sweaty cooks barked orders and stirred huge pans. Amongst the clatter and chaos, Arjun was just another servant boy.

'Through the far doors,' the Cricket told him. 'Quick!'

They entered an enormous dining room. Thirty rows of sumptuously laid tables, each seating over two hundred people. A golden throne on a raised platform, dominating even this vast space.

'Wow,' said Arjun. 'That's some throne.'

'Majestic,' said the Cricket. 'And yours…'

'Once,' replied Arjun.

He hurried past the tables, where a set of intricately carved wooden doors sat open. Beyond them lay another corridor.

'Go right, to the stairs,' said the Cricket.

The floor above should have been heavily guarded. Yet not a single guard stood sentry.

'This leads to the Empress' private chambers...'

'Where are the guards?' asked Arjun.

'Busy outside,' the Cricket replied. 'They won't suspect anyone of wandering the palace. No one would dare.'

'And if we get stopped?'

'Then we're done for,' said the Cricket. 'Well, you are...'

'I'm going to crush you under my foot when we're through,' said Arjun.

'We'll see,' said the Cricket. 'Let's just concentrate on staying alive, shall we?'

They found the poison hidden in a side table.

'She drinks wine,' the Cricket said. 'Just before she addresses the crowds. From a ceremonial chalice.'

'I still don't understand how we'll get away with it,' said Arjun.

'I told you,' said the Cricket.

'And I'm still not sure I want to kill her,' Arjun added. 'She is my sister after all.'

'She'll be reincarnated,' the Cricket replied. 'So, technically she won't be dead. Not for long, anyway...'

The chalice sat by the golden throne. Gilded and set with precious stones, it was rumoured to be priceless.

It had already been filled, and Arjun wasted no time in adding the poison.

'There,' he said. 'Now, do we just wait?'

'No,' replied the Cricket. 'We have to be there…'

'But you didn't mention that earlier,' Arjun protested.

'No, I didn't,' said the Cricket. 'I never reveal everything. Assassin's code. Now, hurry up. It's nearly time!'

It led Arjun to the lower floor, into the palace court. The walls were draped with thick navy velvet curtains, the floor inlaid with gold leaf. A second, less ostentatious throne dominated this room too. Set above the floor, so that visitors stood below the Empress. To the front was the Royal Balcony.

'She's remodelled,' said the Cricket. 'It's awful.'

'Hurry up!' said Arjun, as voices drew nearer.

'Behind the curtains,' said the Cricket. 'The balcony has side rooms. The doors are set into the walls.'

Arjun managed to catch a glimpse of the entourage before hiding. The Royal Guard – elite and deadly. Behind them came the Empress, flanked by two servant girls and a harassed-looking official carrying a scroll.

'Hurry,' said the Cricket.

As Arjun edged around the wall, the sweltering heat and enclosed space caused him to perspire.

'We're going to die,' he whispered. 'What am I even doing here?'

'Relax,' said the Cricket. 'I've never failed.'

'Yes, but I'm not you.'

'Just do what I say,' said the Cricket. 'And stop whining. It doesn't suit a soon-to-be Emperor.'

Finally, a wooden door appeared, and Arjun went through, relieved at the sudden rush of air. The side room opened onto the balcony, through a narrow archway.

'What now?' asked Arjun.

'Now you fulfil your destiny,' said the Cricket. 'The Prime Minister will introduce her and then it's on.'

'But…'

A trumpet fanfare drowned out his voice. As the Empress stepped onto the balcony, the crowds below cheered without conviction. The Prime Minister stepped forward with the scroll.

'Her Majesty, the Empress!' he bellowed.

He unwound the scroll and bowed. The Empress was tall with sharp features and dark eyes. She wore a flowing silvery gown and a simple tiara. Her expression spoke of regal assurance and a hint of distaste.

'Bring forth the chalice!' the man ordered.

A servant girl emerged holding the wine. She knelt and offered the cup.

'Hail Empress,' she said.

The Empress held the chalice above her head. Thirty cannons boomed at once and the crowd listlessly cheered once more.

'Here we go,' said the Cricket.

As the echo of cannon fire faded, the Empress drank deeply. Instantly, her expression turned to shock. She gasped and kicked out, sending the servant girl sprawling.

The chalice fell from her hands

'POISON!' she screeched.

'NOW!' said the Cricket.

Arjun rushed onto the balcony and picked up the cup. The Empress gasped for words, but the poison worked quickly.

'Hello again, dear sister,' Arjun whispered.

'NO!' she croaked.

Arjun held the chalice aloft and turned to the crowd. The Cricket rested on his shoulder. Above them flapped expansive wings. As the Royal Guard rushed towards them, sabres drawn murderously, the crowd began to murmur.

'NO!' cried the Prime Minister, holding back the guards. 'LOOK!'

His eyes had grown wide with shock, his skin pale.

'IT IS THE PROPHECY..!' he gasped.

An enormous bird landed on the balcony's handrail. Its purple feathers were tipped with gold, its eyes sapphire. Opening its crimson beak, it addressed the crowds with a mighty voice.

'BEHOLD!' it said. 'THE PROPHECY TOLD OF A BOY AND A CRICKET. A BOY WHO WOULD BECOME EMPEROR..!'

Below them, the huge crowds had fallen silent. Many were on their knees, holding up their hands in praise.

'PROPHECY HAS BEEN FULFILLED,' the Magic Bird declared. 'ALL HAIL THE BOY EMPEROR!'

Sweeping an enormous wing aside in reverence, it bowed and addressed Arjun.

'*YOUR MAJESTY...*'

Roars erupted from the crowds. They cheered and clapped and many danced in joy. Chants of 'The Prophecy Has Come True' rang around the palace complex.

Arjun could not speak. He took in the crowds and the huge magical bird. The guards were on their knees, holding up their sabres. The Prime Minister knelt too, hands clasped together. Arjun stood dazed. Dare he believe in the unfolding drama? Was this all just another dream?

'What now?' he asked the Cricket.

Only the insect had vanished. A slight young woman stood beside him. She smiled and bowed.

'Your Majesty,' she said. 'Permit me to introduce myself. I am Deven...'

'But you're a *woman*,' said Arjun.

'Last time I checked I was a cricket,' said Deven. 'But, yes, I *am* a woman...'

The Magic Bird grunted with begrudging respect.

'You fulfilled your quest then?' it said.

'Of course,' said Deven. 'I *never* fail.'

Arjun cleared his throat.

'What do I do now?' he asked.

The Magic Bird chuckled.

'Tell them to enjoy the party,' it said, nodding at the crowds. 'We'll sort the rest out later. I'm hungry...'

'Me too,' said Deven.

Several days later, Mrs Bhag returned from market with a street girl in tow.

'Meet the new help,' she told Mr Bhag. 'She's sullen and dirty. Nothing a bath and a good thrashing won't fix…'

The girl blinked at the Bhags.

'But I'm the Empress,' she whispered. 'I'm not meant to be here…'

'Oh dear,' said Mrs Bhag, picking up a rolling pin. 'Another deluded wretch. Seems the bath will have to wait…'

• • •

'The Boy & The Cricket' was commissioned by the young writers of Harborne Academy, Birmingham: Zuhair, Mohamed, William, Isabelle, Endry, Kodie, Aliyah, Izwi, Khyra, Andreja, Yoonis, Zahraa, Ilham, Amir and Omar.

Teachers: Mr Andrew Farrell and Mrs Samera Dhansey.

ABOUT THE AUTHOR

Bali Rai has written over forty novels about teenagers and children. Born in Leicester, his writing is inspired by his working-class, multicultural background. A leading voice in UK teen fiction, Bali is a passionate advocate of libraries, reading for pleasure and promoting literacy. He has nearly twenty years of experience in working with young people across the UK and further afield, and is extremely popular with schools. He has been nominated for and won numerous awards since 2001.

Bali has worked closely with The Reading Agency, Booktrust, The National Literacy Trust , Empathy Lab UK and many other organisations, and was awarded an honorary doctorate by De Montfort University in 2014. He also featured on BBC1's Rebel Writers show and is an ambassador/patron for several high-profile literacy and arts projects. He was a Costa Book Award judge for 2019/20 and is currently working on two new titles. His most recent books are *Now or Never: A Dunkirk Story*, published by Scholastic in 2019, and *Mohinder's War*, published by Bloomsbury in 2020.

BALI SAYS:

I was intrigued by the Read On commission, wondering how it might work and what I could bring to the table. One of the biggest challenges as an author is forging a workable plot from often quite disparate ideas and musings. Read On was an even greater challenge. Mr Farrell and the pupils at Harborne Academy were brilliant, and I came away with a notebook full of themes and ideas. From prophecies to ancient but less well-known mythology, to reincarnation and deja-vu. They also threw in a magical bird and a dark ending, not to mention a talking cricket! Quite a task…

Having said that, the process was great fun. I loved the challenge of coming up with a plot, and trying to fit most of the themes and ideas into it. It's a great way to stretch yourself as a writer, even a professional one like myself. You find ways of resolving plot issues and holes, and incorporating the weird and the downright surreal. My story is dark and silly, and although it didn't use every idea noted, managed to cram in most. I am delighted and honoured to be part of Harborne Academy's participation in the book and cannot wait to see the end result!

AN EXTRACT FROM

Pride and Prejudice

Jane Austen

Elizabeth's spirits soon rising to playfulness again, she wanted Mr. Darcy to account for his having ever fallen in love with her. 'How could you begin?' said she. 'I can comprehend your going on charmingly, when you had once made a beginning; but what could set you off in the first place?'

'I cannot fix on the hour, or the spot, or the look, or the words, which laid the foundation. It is too long ago. I was in the middle before I knew that I *had* begun.'

'My beauty you had early withstood, and as for my manners – my behaviour to *you* was at least always bordering on the uncivil, and I never spoke to you without rather wishing to give you pain than not. Now be sincere; did you admire me for my impertinence?'

'For the liveliness of your mind, I did.'

'You may as well call it impertinence at once. It was very little less. The fact is, that you were sick of civility, of deference, of officious attention. You were disgusted with the women who were always speaking, and looking, and thinking for *your* approbation alone. I roused, and interested you, because I was so unlike *them*. Had you not been really amiable, you would have hated me for it; but in spite of the pains you took to disguise yourself, your feelings were always noble and just; and in your heart, you thoroughly despised the persons who so assiduously courted you. There – I have saved you the trouble of accounting for it; and really, all things considered, I begin to think it perfectly reasonable. To be sure, you knew no actual good of me – but nobody thinks of *that* when they fall in love.'

'Was there no good in your affectionate behaviour to Jane while she was ill at Netherfield?'

'Dearest Jane! Who could have done less for her? But make a virtue of it by all means. My good qualities are under your protection, and you are to exaggerate them as much as possible; and, in return, it belongs to me to find occasions for teasing and quarrelling with you as often as may be; and I shall begin directly by asking you what made you so unwilling to come to the point at last. What made you so shy of me, when you first called, and afterwards dined here? Why, especially, when you called, did you look as if you did not care about me?'

'Because you were grave and silent, and gave me no encouragement.'

'But I was embarrassed.'

'And so was I.'

'You might have talked to me more when you came to dinner.'

'A man who had felt less, might.'

'How unlucky that you should have a reasonable answer to give, and that I should be so reasonable as to admit it! But I wonder how long you *would* have gone on, if you had been left to yourself. I wonder when you *would* have spoken, if I had not asked you! My resolution of thanking you for your kindness to Lydia had certainly great effect. *Too much*, I am afraid; for what becomes of the moral, if our comfort springs from a breach of promise? for I ought not to have mentioned the subject. This will never do.'

'You need not distress yourself. The moral will be perfectly fair. Lady Catherine's unjustifiable endeavours to separate us were the means of removing all my doubts. I am not indebted for my present happiness to your eager desire of expressing your gratitude. I was not in a humour to wait for any opening of yours. My aunt's intelligence had given me hope, and I was determined at once to know every thing.'

'Lady Catherine has been of infinite use, which ought to make her happy, for she loves to be of use. But tell me, what did you come down to Netherfield for? Was it merely to ride to Longbourn and be embarrassed? Or had you intended any more serious consequence?'

'My real purpose was to see *you*, and to judge, if I could, whether I might ever hope to make you love me. My avowed one, or what I avowed to myself, was to see whether your sister were still partial to Bingley, and if she were, to make the confession to him which I have since made.'

'Shall you ever have courage to announce to Lady Catherine what is to befall her?'

'I am more likely to want more time than courage, Elizabeth. But it ought to be done, and if you will give me a sheet of paper, it shall be done directly.'

'And if I had not a letter to write myself, I might sit by you and admire the evenness of your writing, as another young lady once did. But I have an aunt, too, who must not be longer neglected.'

• • •

Chosen by the young writers in the Italian branch of the Read On family.

Erica Bombarda, 17 years old, commented: 'Kindness, thoughtfulness, elegance: Elizabeth and Mr. Darcy's actions reveal a sincere and noble love, that goes beyond social differences, beyond family prejudices, and beyond the obstacles of the nineteenth century.'

AN EXTRACT FROM

Wuthering Heights

Emily Bronte

'There are many things to be considered before that question can be answered properly,' I said, sententiously. 'First and foremost, do you love Mr. Edgar?'

'Who can help it? Of course I do,' she answered.

Then I put her through the following catechism: for a girl of twenty-two it was not injudicious.

'Why do you love him, Miss Cathy?'

'Nonsense, I do – that's sufficient.'

'By no means; you must say why?'

'Well, because he is handsome, and pleasant to be with.'

'Bad!' was my commentary.

'And because he is young and cheerful.'

'Bad, still.'

'And because he loves me.'

'Indifferent, coming there.'

'And he will be rich, and I shall like to be the greatest woman of the neighbourhood, and I shall be proud of having such a husband.'

'Worst of all. And now, say how you love him?'

'As everybody loves – you're silly, Nelly.'

'Not at all – answer.'

'I love the ground under his feet, and the air over his head, and everything he touches, and every word he says. I love all his looks, and all his actions, and him entirely and altogether. There now!'

'And why?'

'Nay; you are making a jest of it: it is exceedingly ill-natured! It's no jest to me!' said the young lady, scowling, and turning her face to the fire.

'I'm very far from jesting, Miss Catherine,' I replied. 'You love Mr. Edgar because he is handsome, and young, and cheerful, and rich, and loves you. The last, however, goes for nothing: you would love him without that, probably; and with it you wouldn't, unless he possessed the four former attractions.'

'No, to be sure not: I should only pity him – hate him, perhaps, if he were ugly, and a clown.'

'But there are several other handsome, rich young men in the world: handsomer, possibly, and richer than he is. What should hinder you from loving them?'

'If there be any, they are out of my way: I've seen none like Edgar.'

'You may see some; and he won't always be handsome, and young, and may not always be rich.'

'He is now; and I have only to do with the present. I wish you would speak rationally.'

'Well, that settles it: if you have only to do with the present, marry Mr. Linton.'

'I don't want your permission for that – I *shall* marry him: and yet you have not told me whether I'm right.'

'Perfectly right; if people be right to marry only for the present. And now, let us hear what you are unhappy about. Your brother will be pleased; the old lady and gentleman will not object, I think; you will escape from a disorderly, comfortless home into a wealthy, respectable one; and you love Edgar, and Edgar loves you. All seems smooth and easy: where is the obstacle?'

'*Here!* And *here!*' replied Catherine, striking one hand on her forehead, and the other on her breast: 'In whichever place the soul lives. In my soul and in my heart, I'm convinced I'm wrong!'

'That's very strange! I cannot make it out.'

'It's my secret. But if you will not mock at me, I'll explain it: I can't do it distinctly; but I'll give you a feeling of how I feel.'

She seated herself by me again: her countenance grew sadder and graver, and her clasped hands trembled.

'Nelly, do you never dream queer dreams?' she said, suddenly, after some minutes' reflection.

'Yes, now and then,' I answered.

'And so do I. I've dreamt in my life dreams that have stayed with me ever after, and changed my ideas: they've gone through and through me, like wine through water, and altered the colour of my mind. And this is one: I'm going to tell it – but take care not to smile at any part of it.'

'Oh! Don't, Miss Catherine!' I cried. 'We're dismal enough without conjuring up ghosts and visions to perplex us. Come, come, be merry and like yourself! Look at little Hareton! *He's* dreaming nothing dreary. How sweetly he smiles in his sleep!'

'Yes; and how sweetly his father curses in his solitude! You remember him, I daresay, when he was just such another as that chubby thing: nearly as young and innocent. However, Nelly, I shall oblige you to listen: it's not long; and I've no power to be merry to-night.'

'I won't hear it, I won't hear it!' I repeated, hastily.

I was superstitious about dreams then, and am still; and Catherine had an unusual gloom in her aspect, that made me dread something from which I might shape a prophecy, and foresee a fearful catastrophe. She was vexed, but she did not proceed. Apparently taking up another subject, she recommenced in a short time.

'If I were in heaven, Nelly, I should be extremely miserable.'

'Because you are not fit to go there,' I answered. 'All sinners would be miserable in heaven.'

'But it is not for that. I dreamt once that I was there.'

'I tell you I won't hearken to your dreams, Miss Catherine! I'll go to bed,' I interrupted again.

She laughed, and held me down; for I made a motion to leave my chair.

'This is nothing,' cried she: 'I was only going to say that heaven did not seem to be my home; and I broke my heart with weeping to come back to earth; and the angels were so angry that they flung me out into the middle of the heath on the top of Wuthering Heights; where I woke sobbing for joy. That will do to explain my secret, as well as the other. I've no more business to marry Edgar Linton than I have to be in heaven; and if the wicked man in there had not brought Heathcliff so low, I shouldn't have thought of it. It would degrade me to marry Heathcliff now; so he shall never know how I love him: and that, not because he's handsome, Nelly, but because he's more myself than I am. Whatever our souls are made of, his and mine are the same; and Linton's is as different as a moonbeam from lightning, or frost from fire.'

'Ere this speech ended I became sensible of Heathcliff's presence. Having noticed a slight movement, I turned my head, and saw him rise from the bench, and steal out noiselessly. He had listened till he heard Catherine say it would degrade her to marry him, and then he stayed to hear no further. My companion, sitting on the ground, was prevented by the back of the settle from remarking his presence or departure; but I started, and bade her hush!

'Why?' she asked, gazing nervously round.

'Joseph is here,' I answered, catching opportunely the roll of his cartwheels up the road; 'and Heathcliff will come in with him. I'm not sure whether he were not at the door this moment.'

'Oh, he couldn't overhear me at the door!' said she. 'Give me Hareton, while you get the supper, and when it is ready ask me to sup with you. I want to cheat my uncomfortable conscience, and be convinced that Heathcliff has no notion of these things. He has not, has he? He does not know what being in love is!'

'I see no reason that he should not know, as well as you,' I returned; 'and if you are his choice, he'll be the most unfortunate creature that ever was born! As soon as you become Mrs. Linton, he loses friend, and love, and all! Have you considered how you'll bear the separation, and how he'll bear to be quite deserted in the world? Because, Miss Catherine –'

'He quite deserted! We separated!' she exclaimed, with an accent of indignation. 'Who is to separate us, pray? They'll meet the fate of Milo! Not as long as I live, Ellen: for no mortal creature. Every Linton on the face of the earth might melt into nothing before I could consent to forsake Heathcliff. Oh, that's not what I intend – that's not what I mean! I shouldn't be Mrs. Linton were such a price demanded! He'll be as much to me as he has been all his lifetime. Edgar must shake off his antipathy, and tolerate him, at least. He will, when he learns my true feelings towards him. Nelly, I see now you think me a selfish wretch; but did it never strike you that if Heathcliff and I married, we should be beggars? Whereas, if I marry Linton I can aid Heathcliff to rise, and place him out of my brother's power.'

'With your husband's money, Miss Catherine?' I asked. 'You'll find him not so pliable as you calculate upon: and, though I'm hardly a judge, I think that's the worst motive you've given yet for being the wife of young Linton.'

'It is not,' retorted she; 'it is the best! The others were the satisfaction of my whims: and for Edgar's sake, too, to satisfy him. This is for the sake of one who comprehends in his person my feelings to Edgar and myself. I cannot express it; but surely you and everybody have a notion that there is or should be an existence of yours beyond you. What were the use of my creation, if I were entirely contained here? My great miseries in this world have been Heathcliff's miseries, and I watched and felt each from the beginning: my great thought in living is himself. If all else perished, and *he* remained, *I* should still continue to be; and if all else remained, and he were annihilated, the universe would turn to a mighty stranger: I should not seem a part of it. My love for Linton is like the foliage in the woods: time will change it, I'm well aware, as winter changes the trees. My love for Heathcliff resembles the eternal rocks beneath: a source of little visible delight, but necessary. Nelly, I *am* Heathcliff! He's always, always in my mind: not as a pleasure, any more than I am always a pleasure to myself, but as my own being. So don't talk of our separation again: it is impracticable; and –'

She paused, and hid her face in the folds of my gown; but I jerked it forcibly away. I was out of patience with her folly!

'If I can make any sense of your nonsense, Miss,' I said,

'it only goes to convince me that you are ignorant of the duties you undertake in marrying; or else that you are a wicked, unprincipled girl. But trouble me with no more secrets: I'll not promise to keep them.'

'You'll keep that?' she asked, eagerly.

'No, I'll not promise,' I repeated.

. . .

Sofia Dal Ry, 17 years old, commented: 'This work describes the confused and troubled feelings of the protagonist, Catherine, who, after making an important decision, expresses her worries and regret.'

Chiara Fiorio, 18 years old, commented: 'Because she manages to give shape in words of disarming power to a feeling that is difficult to define. Catherine's declaration of love reveals all the yearning and urgency of a love that goes beyond any logic and form of will.'

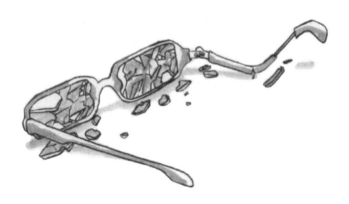

The Greatest Love of All

Sandra Carvalho

Translated from Portuguese by Beth Fowler

I still remember that day clearly. Who could forget. I had left behind my home, my friends, my stomping grounds... I felt so unhappy! In the front of the car, my father sat in silence, not lifting his eyes from the motorway. My mother was twisting round to look at me in the back, wearing my patience thin by repeating for the thousandth time with forced enthusiasm: 'You're going to love the new house! And don't worry, it won't take you long to make friends. Our neighbours have a daughter your age, she's so nice and sweet...' *Yes*, I thought scornfully. *And she's going to love meeting me, because I'm every girl's dream!*

Suddenly there was a bang, like an explosion… One of the cars in front of us skidded off the road and rolled over. It all happened so quickly, but I thought I saw something black being flung into the distance. Then chaos descended as my father hit the brake. I closed my eyes and held my breath, strangled by the seatbelt. I heard the deafening sound of skidding tyres merging with the shriek of metal, and I realised that the car was spinning. Then a dreadful silence overwhelmed my senses. I was wondering if I was dead when my mother cried out in distress, 'Sebastião, darling… Are you all right?'

The anger I felt towards them for having forced such an abrupt life change on me dissolved in a close embrace. We had escaped unhurt, thanks to my father's skill and cool head. Unfortunately the others hadn't been so lucky. The police came quickly, when we had barely recovered our breath. A fleet of emergency vehicles soon followed. Several cars had crashed behind the first, but because we had been ordered to stay in our car we didn't know the extent of the tragedy. My mother watched me like a hawk, afraid I might have a panic attack. That hadn't happened for a while, but the psychologist had warned that an extreme situation could trigger a fresh episode… And this was certainly an extreme situation! But, against all odds, I didn't feel overwhelmed by fear. An officer came to take our details, and I didn't even stammer when I told him I saw something being thrown from the car. He made a note of it and sent us on our way. As we passed the ambulances, my mother begged me not to look. I obeyed without protest. Never before had the expression *carpe diem* made so much sense to me.

In the new house, my room had more than enough space for my books and games, and it caught the morning light. These benefits, however, in no way made up for the ordeal of starting at a school that was cold and hostile compared to the welcoming school I had been forced to leave so that my parents were closer to their respective jobs. As soon as I walked through the door, I made for the library, wanting to minimise my discomfort. That would be where I found my future friends. I was frustrated to find there was no reading club at the school. That said a lot about the natives, who I would have to hang out with for the next two years.

I returned to the playground to brood. The space had filled up and everyone was looking at me like I was a fly in their soup. I forced myself to smile, but no one smiled back. There was still a long time until the bell rang for lessons to start. I leant against the wall of the gym hall and watched the boys and girls joking around together in groups. I remained alone. At my old school, I would have been the first to welcome a new pupil. Here, no one was available to greet me; no one interested in asking my name. I lowered my head and my fringe fell to hide my face. Whenever I peeked out from behind that long dark curtain, I got a feeling of safety, as though my hair had the gift of turning me invisible. It was an instinctively defensive gesture… Complete nonsense, given that some-one my height could never go unnoticed!

Time was dragging painfully... until I saw her. She was alone too, but by choice. Her classmates tried to get her to join them, but she held off. Her freckled face was lit up by her enthusiasm for the book she was holding as if it were like a precious jewel. She had red hair... She was beautiful like a goddess! A goddess with a book! *An oasis in the middle of this arid desert!* I took a step towards her... Then, at my shoulder, a mocking, strident voice sang out:

'Sebastião eats everything, everything, everything. Sebastião eats everything, and all without a spoon...'

It just wasn't possible! After all these years... I turned around slowly, my guts tying themselves in knots. Batman has the Joker. Spiderman has Green Goblin. Superman has Lex Luthor... And I have Dinis Costa! I opened my mouth, completely floored, unable to believe my eyes. But before I could make a sound, one of his large hands was pulling at my shirt, the other clenched in a fist heading straight for my stomach.

We had been in the same class at primary school. In those years, the worst of my life, there wasn't a day when Dinis didn't humiliate me. He was the football ace; I was the fat kid who enjoyed reading. I started wearing contact lenses after he broke my glasses. Of course, I told my parents I had broken them falling off my bike! My beloved bike had often served to justify the bruises on my body, until the day my mum forbade me from using it because I was 'clumsy and easily distracted,' and she had donated it to charity. No, I never told my parents that I was Dinis's punchbag. Only when my panic attacks

97

started did they suspect that I might be the victim of bullying. But it was around then that Dinis's parents decided to move away, and I never heard of the beast again… Until now! At that moment, I was at the mercy of his strength and, though he had barely pushed his fist into my stomach, just simulating a punch, I felt a real pain, a consequence of the terrible memories haunting me.

'Sebastião's a pot-bellied pig. And that's why it's fun to punch him!' the idiot crooned, encouraged by a chorus of laughter. I swallowed the tears that sprang to my eyes. I wasn't going to panic! Dinis was no longer much stronger than I was! I plucked up my courage and freed myself with a shove. Irritated, he attacked with twice the resentment… This time, the punch would be unforgiving!

'How's it going, Dinis?'

A girl's voice made him step aside hurriedly and his fist missed my nose by millimetres. He started to hop about, throwing punches in the air as though he were at boxing training, and replied: 'It's all good, Rita! I'm just playing!'

My cheeks nearly exploded with shame before this red-haired goddess. Her smile broadened and she asked innocently, 'Is the new boy a friend of yours?'

Dinis was embarrassed. 'No! You really think I'd be friends with this *luzzer*?' he said, mispronouncing the English word.

The goddess stared at me and replied in a critical tone, 'Actually, an ignoramus like you would never be friends with a *loser*!' I stood open mouthed. As well as correcting his terrible English, had she also stood up to him? But

Dinis was laughing and his obliging friends patted him on the back, lavishing the usual praise. The bell echoed and they moved away. The goddess faced me. 'For your own good, you'd better wise up sharpish!' she said, sternly.

I wanted to thank her, but she turned away, uninterested. I tried again: 'Wait… Was Dinis actually pleased that you called him an ignoramus?' Rita stopped, surprised that I had noticed.

'The idiot thought I was praising him… These imbeciles have never even heard of a dictionary. And just as well! That way I can be imaginative with my insults.' *And voila*, I thought. *I'm in love!*

A teacher interrupted us and sent us to our classrooms. What a shame Rita wasn't in my class… Darn it, if I didn't run I'd be marked absent! I climbed the stairs from the gym hall, my lungs bursting, repeating: *Dinis can't be in my class…*

'Dinis Costa is in my class,' I grumbled, when my mother asked how my day had been. She trawled through her memory and smiled.

'I didn't know the Costas had returned from France. Are they living here? That's nice! You see? You've already got a friend at school!'

I felt like shouting. Sometimes I got the impression that my parents didn't know the first thing about me… They made no effort to know! My mother couldn't guess that Dinis had tormented me in the past, but she must have been able to sense, from my sullen face and my glum tone, that this was not good news. She had already changed the subject, though. 'I went to give my statement about the crash on the motorway… In the car that overturned, there was a couple with their daughter. The parents died and the girl is in hospital.' It made me feel bad to recall how frightened we had been. Back in my room, to distract myself, I started thinking about the redheaded goddess. What book had she been reading? I hoped it was one of my favourites! That way, I'd have the chance to make a good impression when I spoke to her. But when I lay down, the memory of the accident came back to upset me. I murmured prayer for the girl in hospital and that soothed me a bit. When I finished, I fell asleep.

The class had assembled to wait for the Portuguese teacher, and Dinis didn't tire of tormenting me.

'Make way for Lardboy, the fatty who munches on lard for breakfast!' His bootlickers laughed, but some of the pupils rolled their eyes, annoyed. Perhaps there were some friendly faces in that crowd of idiots after all!

The teacher arrived, smiling, and put an end to the torture. We had barely sat down when she explained the reason for her enthusiasm: 'This year, I'm going to give you the opportunity to do a project on a book you like… Any book at all, it's your choice!'

The bored sighs of some of the class mingled with the applause of others. I was satisfied, until she revealed in a jokey tone: 'As an even bigger treat, you're going to do an oral presentation!'

We all exchanged looks of indignation and horror. Then the protests thundered in unison, until the teacher cut them off.

'If you continue to express your 'joy' like this, I'm going to add some more 'creative ideas' to the project!' In the blink of an eye, silence engulfed the room. The teacher was nice, but she turned cruel when she was annoyed. The lesson started and, gradually, everyone seemed to forget about the assignment… except for me!

An oral presentation… That's all I need! I pondered fearfully, my stomach doing somersaults. I lowered my head so that my fringe hid my face. *How am I going to speak in front of all these strangers? Dinis will make fun of me until the cows come home!* I only realised that the teacher had called on me several times when she shouted my name. I swiftly turned to face her and nervously met her angry eye.

'Could you explain to me what is more important than the lesson, Sebastião?' I desperately wanted a hole to open in the floor and swallow me up. I tried to apologise, but my tongue was stuck.

All of a sudden, she decided: 'Sebastião will be the first to give his presentation… And anyone else who thinks it isn't worth paying attention in my class will be next.' My heart contracted and bile burned my throat. Nauseated, I realised that I was about to suffer a panic attack. Fortunately, the bell rang just then. I ran wildly from the room. If I didn't get away from everyone and everything, I wouldn't be able to control myself.

I ran and ran, until my strength gave out, overwhelmed by a suffocating anguish, completely disoriented. When I came to my senses I was on a plot of open wasteland, far away from the school. I was recovering my breath when a girl appeared.

'Sebastião, come quickly!'

I stared at her, astonished. She seemed to be about my age and she was pretty, with long black hair and green eyes set off by the white of her dress. How did she know my name?

'Come on! Only you can save him!' Her desperation persuaded me to follow her. She said her name was Maria... There was no time for anything else. In front of us, cowering under the parched branches of a bush, was a small dog, and it was in a bad way.

'What kind of lowlife could do this to an animal?' I breathed, horrified.

'Help him, please!' begged Maria, explaining that she couldn't pick him up.

'We need to take him to a vet,' I decided.

The dog yelped weakly when I touched him. He had a nice collar, with 'Toy' written on it, so he must have had an owner. I thought it was the perfect name for that black ball of fluff with a white stain above his nose.

'Relax, Toy,' I murmured as I picked him up, afraid he might bite me. But despite the pain, his black eyes stared at me with gratitude when I nestled him under the protection of my arm.

'There's a vet nearby,' urged Maria. So we returned to

the streets of the town, her running ahead of me, swift as a cheetah. People looked at us curiously, but no one bothered to offer to help. I turned a corner and came across the door of the veterinary surgery... But where was Maria? Had she gone inside? No. Confused, I handed the dog to the nurse and hurried to call my mother.

Toy didn't have an identification chip, so it would be impossible to find his owner if they weren't looking for him. He was starving and dehydrated, and he had several broken ribs and had lost a lot of blood. The vet's opinion was that he had been run over and, in shock, he had run aimlessly until exhaustion forced him to stop. A few more hours without getting help and he would have died. My mother felt so sorry for him that she agreed to take him home until he was healed.

'But if the owner doesn't show up, we'll have to give him to a dog home so that another family can adopt him. You know your father doesn't like animals!' I didn't mention Maria, in case my mother got angry at her for abandoning Toy... In any case, I probably wouldn't see her again.

The week was coming to an end and Dinis was still making my life a living hell. No one in the class dared speak to me, afraid of what Dinis might do. Rita nodded to me sometimes but I didn't try talking to her, in case Dinis put me down in front of her again. The last class of the day was Portuguese. I entered nervously; choosing a book to present next week was proving difficult. It had to be one with a gripping plot, so it would help me get a good grade. I sat down at the back of the class, hoping the teacher wouldn't notice me. I was keen to get home and play with Toy... Finally I had a dog, something I'd always dreamed of! But that happiness was hanging by a thread. Toy was almost better and my father was immoveable in his decision to give him to a dog home. Curiously, perhaps because Toy sensed that my father was the leader of his 'new pack', he followed him everywhere with a look of adoration. Sadly, this didn't improve the situation, much to my sorrow and my mother's self-confessed grief.

The class was never-ending! I looked out across the playground impatiently and my heart began to race as I saw Rita sitting on a bench, devouring the final pages of her mysterious book. I still hadn't discovered...

'It's *Harry Potter and the Philosopher's Stone*,' said a gentle voice from the other side of the window. Startled, I leant out to find out who had read my mind, and I almost yelped in alarm when I came face to face with Maria. Suddenly, my name echoed in my ears, with a chilling sensation of déjà vu. My eyes turned to meet the teacher's, like metal attracted by a powerful magnet.

'What's the book, Sebastião?'

Stunned, I replied, '*Harry Potter and the Philosopher's Stone*...' The kids burst out laughing.

'Silence!' ordered the teacher, adding: 'All right. It will be an interesting presentation.'

'What? No... No!' I was horrified to realise what was happening.

'Are you messing with me, Sebastião?' The teacher's exasperated tone made me freeze.

'Sorry...' And I shut up. My fate was sealed.

This cannot be happening to me! I agonised, standing at the bookshop window. I was purple with shame just thinking about buying the stupid book... I would die when I had to present it to the class!

'Cheer up, Sebastião! There's nothing like a fantasy story to stimulate the imagination... And it's imagination that feeds our dreams, and allows us to create original and wonderful things!' Stunned, I turned to see Maria. Had she had the nerve to follow me to the shopping centre to preach at me?

'Well, I hate fantasy! And now, because of you, I'm going to have to read a ridiculous kids' book!'

She just replied: 'How is it my fault that you chose the book Rita is reading?'

She went into the bookshop. I followed her reluctantly. I waited until we were alone, so that no one would see me buy that rubbish. The assistant, who must have thought I was planning to rob the shop, gave me an unfriendly look when I placed the book on the counter.

Embarrassed, I stuttered: 'It isn't for me! It's a present... for my sister!' I pointed at Maria. She'd better not deny it! From the corner of my eye, I saw her nod in confirmation, but the man kept looking at me, as if she were invisible and I was crazy. As soon as we left, Maria burst out laughing.

'You made a fool of yourself!'

'Or the book is terrible and the guy was making fun of me,' I fretted. I was going to ask her why she had left me alone the other day, when she pointed ahead.

'There's Rita!' Adrenalin flooded my veins. I wanted to slip away, but the redheaded goddess was already approaching with another girl.

'Hi, Sebastião! This is Beatriz.' I controlled my nerves and turned to the side.

'And this is...' I fell silent, dazed. Maria had vanished again! What on earth?!

Rita handed me one of the leaflets she was distributing. 'Tomorrow there's going to be a music and dance performance at the theatre. We're in it.' When they had gone, I looked around for Maria, but once again she had abandoned me for no reason.

I entered the theatre keen to show my goddess that I had come along to support her. My mother was with me, as my father had to work. It didn't take her long to start chatting to the other women... If only I had her easy way of making friends! It was a pleasant auditorium. The lights went down and the stage lit up. Laughter ensued with a play performed by the theatre group. This was followed by a circus act. Then, traditional Fado singers. A magician spread delight and amazement...

'Are you enjoying it?' I was shocked to see Maria sitting on the steps next to my seat. It was incredible, but I couldn't be angry with her!

'Very much so,' I replied.

'That's good, Sebastião! Rita's up next...' On the stage, the magician was saying goodbye. I turned back to the stairs, but, just for a change, Maria had disappeared. I forgot her in an instant, as my goddess made her appearance, her red hair flaming... Dazzling!

'Good evening,' she said into the microphone. 'Tonight I will have the honour of singing 'The Greatest Love of All', by the diva Whitney Houston. But first, I would like to share with you something I wrote, inspired by that theme. To be original, I called it 'The Greatest Love of All'.'

The crowd laughed politely at her joke... Who was this Whitney? My mother seemed to know... I thought about checking Wikipedia, but I stopped myself because Rita had started her speech:

'I came into your world with my heart open and a smile on my lips... But you all rejected the hand I held out to you and you mocked my voice. How magnificent you are, ladies and gentlemen, tall like giants, wise like gods! From the height of your pride, you dug deep rivers around me, you piled mountains in front of me, you set fire to the earth beneath my feet... Nevertheless, I am here! I achieved my destiny, exhausted, but very proud of myself. You were wrong! Your contempt doesn't hurt me; it only gives me greater strength... Because the thorny path I have travelled taught me that the respect and esteem that a human being nourishes for themselves is the greatest love of all... And now, the greatest love of all burns like a magnificent bonfire inside me!'

The applause shattered my astonishment. Rita had expressed herself as though it were some kind of release, a means of overcoming discrimination! She started to sing… And what a beautiful voice she had! She left the stage to a huge ovation. I was still struggling with my confusion when a group of girls took to the stage to dance to 'Jenny of Oldstones'. Beatriz stood out as the best… until Maria joined them. My jaw dropped to see her move among the others with unrivalled grace. She spun, jumped, ran and whirled… She glided through the air, her white dress highlighting the lightness of her movements. Was she attached to a cable? The illusion was so majestic that she seemed to be flying! The dance ended and I clapped enthusiastically. If I had to choose the best performance, Maria would have won! Rita had been phenomenal, but Maria was perfect!

On the way home, my mother praised the performance of the various artists, including Rita. I was surprised she didn't mention Maria, but I stayed quiet so that I wouldn't have to admit how I knew her. I could hardly have imagined that the most wonderful of miracles was still awaiting me that evening. Back home, we caught my father fast asleep on the sofa… snuggled up with Toy! I caught my mother's eye, astonished, and she broke into a broad smile. This could only mean that the puppy had won my father's heart – I felt huge relief and joy. After his near-death experience, Toy had found a family that loved him. He would be very happy dog!

On Sunday, my parents went out for a walk. I stayed at home to start reading Harry Potter, even though I would rather have hit my foot with a hammer. In my bedroom, bored, I remembered my goddess and her excellent performance. It was good to know that Rita also drew inspiration from music. I could only stand Dinis's provocations because I closed my ears and hummed my war songs to myself, songs that helped me through difficult times. I started playing one of them and distracted myself by dancing… Until, after a spin, I noticed Maria watching me, scornfully. My cry of fright merged with her laughter.

'I don't want to be a wet blanket, Seb, but you've got a book to read!'

'How did you get in here?' I asked, sweeping my fringe back from my face. Maria pointed at the open window.

'Can I see Toy?' she begged.

'First you have to explain to me why you're always vanishing,' I said snippily.

'It's complicated… I'm all alone, Seb! My family is far away… Please, don't be angry!' It was crazy, but I could have sworn that Maria was glowing! I lost the will to question her. I opened the door and Toy scampered in, out of his mind with joy. I told Maria my father had agreed that this adorable ball of fur could join our family. She was delighted.

'I'm so glad! I know you'll take good care of him.' Then she pointed at the Harry Potter book.

'Do you want company to start it?'

Annoyed, I confessed: 'That bunch of wizards on the front is putting me off… These famous series annoy me! Everyone has read the books, seen the films and knows the story inside out.'

'That just goes to show that it's a good story.'

'I doubt it!'

'Don't be so against it, Seb! I can guarantee that you're going to like it.' Toy jumped onto the bed and curled up, ready for a nap. I took a deep breath… and gave in to Maria's arguments and the inevitability of the task.

Time flew, largely because of the book, which opened my eyes to a whole new world. It was unbelievable, but I was loving the Harry Potter story! The first few pages were almost painful to get through, and without Maria's encouragement I might have given up at the first chapter. But as soon as I decided to embrace the fantasy, it became hard to stop reading. I found myself euphoric and eager, my emotions running high, going up and down along with Harry's, while I took in every word with amazement and admiration. I was so absorbed that it was only when my parents got home that I realised that Maria had gone.

Later, after I finished the book, I admitted with a lump in my throat that I had read it so quickly because I identified with the main character, in his fight against evil. I was so into the series that I bought the second volume and started to dream that I was part of the story: I became a courageous wizard, I fought glorious battles and defeated my demons… The most extraordinary thing was that these dreams helped me face my fear! I even walked past Dinis without flinching, which discouraged him from spitting out his string of atrocities. I was even ready to talk about the book in class… But then, on the day, the teacher made a surprise announcement:

'The head of department has suggested that you give your presentations in the school auditorium, along with all the other Portuguese classes. You can go there now.'

That was enough to shred all the courage I had plucked up in the meantime. *I'm going to have to speak in front of a hundred people? No! It can't be*! I left the room abruptly, my heart racing, my mind in turmoil and my vision blurring. I knew what was happening to me… *No! I have to control myself… I can't break down in front of them!* Yes, people break too… And I was on the verge of shattering into a million pieces!

Instead of going into the auditorium, I made for the toilets and locked myself in one of the cubicles. I sat down, hugging my knees, gasping for breath, tears spilling down my face as I swayed backwards and forwards and dug my nails into my palms. *I can't do it…* My body had become a shapeless mass, trembling all over. My head was throbbing, my heart threatening to burst and my lungs contracting. I was going to faint…

Suddenly, a bang shook me back to awareness. The toilet door had swung wide open! Dinis's mocking voice struck through my distress right to my soul:

'Sebas… I know you're in here!' I heard the laughter of Vitor, his best friend. They started to thump on the cubicle door. I covered my mouth and shrank into myself even more, panicking. *I don't deserve this!* Suddenly, silence. Could they have given up? No! They returned to attack the door, using a card to try to open it. It worked.

'Slimy Seb is crying!' They dragged me out and threw me down on the freezing floor. I lay there, desperate, at the mercy of their laughter.

'Did you think you could hide from us?' snarled Dinis, spitting on me. 'Let's video this sissy and make him a You-Tube star.' He pulled out his mobile.

But Vitor hesitated. 'Come on, Dinis… That's enough! Leave him in peace!'

'Leave him…?! Are you stupid?!'

'No… It's just… I don't want to get into trouble! My dad's already warned me…'

'Well get lost then! I don't need someone like you anyway!'

I watched the argument between my executioners, paralysed with horror. But when I saw Vitor leave, a flame ignited within me. Dinis had barely pointed his mobile at me when I got up and faced him.

'You think you're the big guy?' I said. 'You're nothing but a coward, thick as mud!' That wouldn't sound so good on the recording.

Furious, Dinis pushed me against the wall, shouting: 'You're going to die…' But before his punch could reach me, he was dragged backwards. Astonished, I saw Maria slapping him across the face. His mobile was tossed into the air, then bounced off a toilet and broke into pieces. Dinis stared at me, his eyes bulging in amazement.

He stammered: 'H… how… did you do that?'

And again, Maria attacked him and, without the slightest bit of fear, squeezed his neck. Certain that Dinis would attack her, I leapt to her defence. But I stopped when I saw him lift his hands to his throat and gasp: 'Stop, Sebastião… Stop…' He fell to his knees in front of Maria, but he continued to stare at me and to gulp, as if he were suffocating: 'Please…' I turned to Maria, puzzled. And this time there was no doubt about it. She was emanating light!

Maria let go of Dinis. He crashed to the floor and retreated, dragging himself along on his buttocks, panting, terrified. As soon as he reached the door, he fled. Convinced that Dinis hadn't seen Maria, I looked at her, aghast.

'Who are you?' I said. Yes, just who was that girl who appeared and disappeared as if bewitched, who shone as if she were covered in magic dust and whom no one else could see? Could she be a real wizard? Or was I delirious?

Maria walked up to me, wrapping me in her deep green gaze and said sweetly: 'You saved my best friend, that's why I wanted to help you… But now I have to go and see my family. Anyway, you don't need me anymore! The flame that sparked in you today will never go out…

'Go on! You have a book to present… Just the first of many challenges you will excel in! When you find Joana,

113

she'll tell you all about me... Be strong, Seb! Be amazing!'

Stunned, I saw her vanish into thin air, as if she were made of shimmering powder that slowly dissipated in a non-existent breeze.

I entered the auditorium with my legs trembling. *Could it have been a hallucination?* I didn't have time to analyse my amazement and incredulity, however, because everyone was there. On the stage, the Portuguese teacher announced:

'Sebastião Rodrigues will present the book *Harry Potter and the Philosopher's Stone*, by J.K. Rowling.'

All eyes turned to me. I started walking forwards, but I hesitated when I saw Dinis. He was whispering to the rest of the class, gesticulating and pointing at me. Unexpectedly, Rita appeared, took my arm and encouraged me to keep going.

'Good choice of book! Go on. I'll help you walk past your Voldemort.'

I refused. 'Dinis is all talk. Shyness and insecurity are my Voldemort... but I'm going to beat them!'

When I reached the stage, I realised that I was sweating profusely. I swept my hair back from my face and swallowed drily, looking at the high ceiling and light flooding through the windows, before plucking up the courage to face the expectant audience. Here and there, I could hear muffled laughter.

'Want us to call an ambulance?' someone joked.

My teacher was losing patience: 'Time is running out,

Sebastião. Your classmates have to do their presentations too...'

I can do this, I thought. *After all, I'm going to talk about a book I love...* I started in a hesitant, hoarse voice, my nerves catching in my throat. But after a few seconds of anguish, I found myself focusing completely. My thoughts flowed smoothly and my voice became firmer. From that moment, time seemed to fly... Suddenly, the presentation was finished and everyone was on their feet applauding, shouting in support! Even my teacher had a big smile.

'Bravo, Sebastião!' she exclaimed. 'I'm proud of your effort!'

'Sebastião Rodrigues: 19.8 out of 20.'

I was ecstatic, staring at my Portuguese teacher. Had I misheard? My classmates got up to high-five me, which made the moment real. I was enveloped in a wave of happiness, as if a warmth was growing in my chest and spreading throughout my body.

With a satisfied expression, the teacher said: 'I want you all to know that this was the best grade out of all the classes. Well done, Sebastião! Your effort and progress were remarkable!' I thanked her, blushing.

Vitor slapped me on the back, lifted my arm and exclaimed: 'Viva Sebastião Potter, the *Winner*!'

The whole class shouted: 'Viva!' And finally, I understood what Rita had meant when she said that there's no greater love than our self-esteem. After I'd overcome the terror of the oral presentation, I had learned to trust in my abilities. I knew instinctively that I wouldn't suffer any more panic attacks, because there were no monsters in my path that the sword of my intelligence and the magic wand of my confidence couldn't defeat.

I came back down to earth and was faced with Dinis's resentful grimace. After the incident in the toilets, he had tried to convince everyone that I was a wizard, that I had attacked him with my abominable powers and nearly killed him. No one believed him! At last, even his friends had had enough of his obsession and started to defend me whenever he insulted me. Despite everything, I didn't feel resentful. On the contrary, I nurtured the hope that, one day, Dinis would have the decency to admit he had been wrong and take back what he had said.

At breaktime, Rita came to congratulate me. The news of my grade had spread through the school like wildfire. She had some good news too: 'Our reading club gained five new members today!' This was a challenge I had put to her after the presentation, and she had accepted immediately. I was glad I had repressed my desire to declare my feelings for her, because that same day I had discovered that Rita and Beatriz were an item.

Rita's outpouring of emotion at the show had been a concealed message to her father and stepmother, fanatical followers of a strange sect, who had thrown her out of the house when she told them she had fallen in love with a girl. Because her mother lived in Australia, Rita was living with her grandparents. To my surprise, I hadn't been upset or sad at this revelation. I still thought Rita was as beautiful as a goddess, but our social contact had proved to me that I was happy just being her friend.

I was looking forward to telling my parents that I had got the best grade in Portuguese. It was incredible how much my life had changed in the last week… partly thanks to Maria! I still didn't know who or what she was, or why she had sought me out, or why she had vanished for good, but I would never forget her. Some heartfelt impulse made me sketch her face in my secret notebook. Modesty aside, it was a great picture! That afternoon, I drew the final touches and, with quickened breath, I wrote in one corner: 'Who is Joana?'

Just then, Toy entered the room and touched me with his paw, a sign that he needed to go out to the street. Since my parents wouldn't be back for a while yet, I took him for a walk in the park. On the way back, as I passed the door of the gym hall, I smiled again to think how much my habits had changed. I had enrolled in karate classes and I was eating better, not because 'Sebastião is big and meaty, Sebastião is always eating,' but because I wanted to feel healthier.

When I got home, I found the neighbours' door open and some suitcases at the entrance. My parents had chatted to them when we moved in, but I hadn't set eyes on them until now. I took a discreet look…

Suddenly, Toy pulled sharply at the leash, tearing off to invade alien territory. Distressed, I ran after him. Then I heard an excited voice shouting:

'Mum, Dad, Toy is here!'

And I came face to face with a girl my age, with long black hair, embracing my dog, with tears in her green eyes.

Shocked, I felt I was simultaneously freezing and burning inside, my heart galloping and my mind in spasm.

'Ma… Maria?' I stammered.

Suddenly, her parents appeared. 'Joana, what was…?' They were surprised to see me. The woman noticed the ball of fluff on her daughter's lap and exclaimed:

'Goodness me, it really is Toy!'

Meanwhile, my parents had arrived home. Everyone said hello. Apparently I was the only one who didn't understand what was going on.

'Toy was Maria's dog,' Joana's mother was saying.

'Sebastião found him on some wasteland,' my mother explained. Aware of my confusion, Joana showed me a photo on her mobile of two very similar girls, her and her cousin Maria, playing with a dog. With Toy! The white stain on his black snout was unmistakeable! *Had I stumbled into a parallel reality..? Could this be a dream? Had I gone crazy!?*

That afternoon, I learnt that not everything in life can be explained by cold hard reason. Maria and her parents had been in the car that overturned in the accident we had witnessed on the motorway. The black thing I had seen thrown into the distance was Toy. Maria's parents had died instantly; she had been in a coma. Joana and her parents, who were Maria's aunt and uncle as well as our neighbours, had barely left the hospital in the hope that Maria would wake up. They only came home to sleep, but I hadn't noticed them. Then, a week ago, on the day of my presentation, Maria's light had gone out. Overcome with grief, the family had taken a short trip to come to terms with it, and were just returning now. Yes, my parents had known all of this, except for Toy's involvement. They had even attended the funerals. I, however, had been kept in the dark so that I wouldn't be traumatised… If only they knew!

In some way, as her body lay in a hospital bed, Maria's spirit had sought me out so that I would save her best friend, Toy. After being thrown from the car, wounded and disoriented, the poor creature must had wandered in search of his owners, until, exhausted, he had lain down to die. If I told my parents all this, they'd cart me off to a psychiatrist in a panic! But I couldn't deceive Joana. When I had called her 'Maria,' she sensed that I was keeping a secret, and she wouldn't rest until I confessed. I showed her the drawing I had made of her cousin and was a shoulder for her compulsive crying.

Maria had said: 'Joana will tell you all about me…' And Joana did! To her, Maria was the most wonderful, generous and tender person who had ever lived.

'Why did she choose me?' I asked her, as we walked Toy in the park.

'Because you're special too, Seb,' she replied. And then she went charmingly red as she added: 'And, maybe, because she knew that the two of us would meet!'

A year later, the Read On project arrived at my school, and each member of the reading club was invited to write a story. Rita is no longer with us, as she moved to the same school as Beatriz. But I'll never forget the lesson she taught me, about the importance of overcoming our fears and insecurities and believing in the strength of our heart. Right away, as soon as I sat down to write this story, a tribute to Maria, the title came to me naturally... Because now, the greatest love of all burns brightly inside me as well!

• • •

'The Greatest Love of All' was commissioned by the young writers of Escola Secundária Emídio Navarro, Almada, Portugal: Gonçalo Jorge, Inês Santos, Joana Rosa, Mariana Takenit, Filipe Santos, Diogo Marques, Ivan Rafael, Sofia Sousa, Tomás Alves, Ângela Nunes.

ABOUT THE AUTHOR

Sandra Carvalho was born in Sesimbra, Portugal, on an old street overlooking the sea. Her love of books from a young age led her to discover new worlds that fired her imagination and encouraged her to write. Today, she is one of the most respected authors of Portuguese fantasy novels, with twelve books published by Editorial Presença, one of which has been translated into Spanish and published in Mexico by Ediciones B, part of Penguin Random House.

Her writing, built on emotions, is notable for its ability to transport readers into her stories, making them visualise the colours and sense the smells and flavours, at the same time as dazzling with the authenticity of her characters.

In 2019, Sandra Carvalho won the Literature prize of the Association of Women Entrepreneurs in Europe & Africa.

Failed encounters

Maria Francisca Macedo

Translated from Portuguese by Beth Fowler

*You've been on my mind since the day I met you
and I don't know why. I'd like you to take away the part of
me that belongs to you. Once and for all.
You know, it hurts to love you. It confuses me.
I've never seen you smile.
I swore to myself that I would make you happy.
This is my story:
about an idiotic boy in love with an unhappy girl.*

The day had started half an hour earlier, but there
was nothing. She walked through the school gates,
and nothing. Her classmates were chatting amongst

themselves: nothing. Joana couldn't feel it, whatever it was. Joana had no mother. No father. No home.

And now, she had no grandmother.

'Are you okay?' her classmate asked. 'Did you hear what we said about this afternoon?'

Joana forced herself to smile as she caught sight of him: Samuel, with his honest gaze, his insightful manner, dazzling with charm and seeming to soothe her internal conflicts.

Samuel.

'Of course. Everyone's going to be there. Beach. After school. Count me in.'

Perhaps he'd be there, with his hair as dark as night and eyes as clear as day, his warm, firm hands and a scent of mystery. Joana felt nothing, she was absent, but when she looked at him, something was there, trying to wake her up.

As if happiness wasn't forbidden to her.

The bell still hadn't rung. Buses arrived and departed. She straightened her backpack as she admired him from afar. She decided it was time to make a move, to ignore her nerves, but she was stalled by a voice she recognised:

'Hi Joana!' She felt her heart leap as she spun to confront the familiar face. She tried to smile quickly. But all she could see when she turned round were the bus headlights announcing her disappointment, by now etched on her pale features.

He was no longer there.

She shook her head and went back to concentrating on her sadness. Class was about to begin.

Everyone thinks I'm insensitive. Useless.
Fernando Pessoa once said that the moment
we intellectualise our feelings, they stop being pure.
They are rationalised emotions, constantly changing,
and therefore easier to mediate.
But I want to feel, truly and genuinely, so I prefer to say
nothing, so that I stay true to myself.

When Joana arrived at the beach, giant waves were smacking against the wet sand, sounds of laughter bursting across the warm summer scene. The light blue sky had a slight pinkish tinge, announcing the sunset, while restless seagulls flew around in droves.

'You should be happy,' she thought. 'Echo. The whole beach is filled with my echo. I'm shouting for help in silence and no one can hear me!'

She saw her cousin and a friend, who waved to her. She waved back, a knot in her stomach: he was there.

As she drew nearer, she laid down her towel before running into the sea. She joined the others with flushed cheeks and greeted everyone, or almost everyone:

'Hey! What about me? Have you forgotten me?' Samuel asked.

She smiled, impatient, as she dived into the water. Slightly put out, he brushed his hair off his face.

'Didn't you hear me?' he asked.

'Yes!' she replied, whirling with satisfaction in the

waves. She was like a butterfly fluttering with a strange, almost exaggerated joy. He shook his head, confused. He loved her. He wanted her. But he couldn't understand her fickleness: she seemed to go from happy to sad so quickly. Perhaps the key was in that word: seemed.

Samuel didn't hesitate. He jumped up and ran into the sea. The huge waves salted his skin.

'It would be nice if you didn't leave me hanging, you know?' he exclaimed, half joking, half very much serious, as he dived after her.

She smiled, this time a genuine smile. As if she were allowed to be happy for brief moments.

'Joana, come on! You haven't spoken to me for months! Not since the day when...'

Her eyes darkened immediately. That day, no. They couldn't talk about *that* day. Her smile vanished and she ran out of the sea. The water streaming from her hair disguised the tears she feared would arrive.

'Darn it,' he thought, standing still in the waves, 'I've messed up again.'

And he watched her flee from the beach.

Night fell quickly. He got up, grabbed his things and left his friends who were still stretched out on the sand. His bicycle was parked on the jetty, at the start of the beach, and he took the opportunity to call his brother on his mobile, for a private word.

'She's so closed off,' he said, grabbing his bike. 'I've tried, but I can't reach her.'

'You have to be patient, you can't let this Natalie Portman lookalike get away that easily!'

Samuel was pedalling by now, and almost dropped his towel as he nestled his mobile between his ear and his shoulder. 'I know, but there's no way of knowing what's going on in her head when she's with me. I just don't get her! She goes from happy to sad in a second flat…'

His brother interrupted.

'Of course you don't! She's a woman! But if you stopped being so shy and opened up to her more, perhaps she would reciprocate.'

My name is Samuel.
My main worry is: what then?
Every time I go to sleep it's the same.
Always the same scenario: a dark corridor, locked doors,
pillars with bizarre drawings, I don't know what's going on.
I hear shouts, or rather – I only hear the shout
of one person, a child, but I couldn't say what age or gender.
But when I try to reach them,
I feel a presence inside me that saps my strength.
I don't know what that presence is or what it wants from me,
but when I collapse the shouts stop for a moment
and I hear strong, heavy breathing, and after a while
I hear the same shout, but much more intense and more
harrowing and then I wake up.
What on earth is happening to me?!
Joana, Joana: the sadness you're hiding
is making me crazy.

It was 7:57 and Joana woke up with light on her face, even though the sky was grey. Drowsy-eyed, she dragged herself out of bed, opened the window and idly looked outside.

A woman on the street caught her eye. She was carrying a jacket over her arm and a flower in in her hand, which Joana imagined she had been given. When the woman turned round, she realised it was her grandmother. She shivered and took a closer look.

Of course it wasn't. That would be impossible.

'I've missed her ever since that day,' she thought. '*That* fateful day.'

It wasn't just that she missed her. She felt an enormous pain, an overwhelming guilt. Sometimes she felt anguished, as if she could never again be happy. As if it would be better to end it all.

'But other times I feel strangely calm, because I can't do it. Because I can't do it for you...'

Leave. See her grandmother once again, the woman who had raised her, been like a mother to her. She pressed her face against the glass, misting it with her tears.

'Oh Grandma... I'm sorry...' The fact that she was sixteen meant that, in the eyes of the law, she was capable of looking after herself now that she had no family. No one to cushion the fall.

'I'm adrift, no direction. It's like I can't feel anything when you're not here. I find it hard to understand my emotions without you to help me.'

Every morning was the same.

It was such a struggle to turn on the light, pretend that everything was fine. That it was all just sadness, just the usual grief.

Joana got dressed on autopilot and returned to school. Yesterday she had been absent again. Or perhaps not, perhaps it had been the weekend. Had she slept too long? It didn't really matter. Today she was going to get dressed and go back to school.

She listened to the luminous silence of the morning echoing through her like a tame bird.

Perhaps today Samuel would notice, perhaps today he would save her.

'Only he can pull me out of the darkness that is my life,' she thought, as she approached the gates, her hair obscuring her brimming eyes. She heard a voice that was like a melody to her soul.

'Hey, I didn't see you at school, is everything okay?'

A feeling of surprise flooded through her, the hope that this concern and attention was sincere and reciprocal.

'It's nothing, I'm just tired,' she replied, wanting him to contradict her. *Please notice. Please, hug me. I'm breaking. Oh, please…*

'Ah, okay,' said the boy, turning round to leave. 'I hope you're feeling better tomorrow.'

She felt as though a truck had run into her and left her unconscious.

No.

Today wasn't the day she would be saved.

It was time to put on her smile again.

'I… I need to speak to you, Samuel,' she said, feigning nonchalance. 'Could we meet on the jetty, after class?'

He nodded without looking at her, scared of replying in some way that might scare the butterfly.

'I finish at five,' said Samuel, and off he went to class. Needless to say, he found it hard to concentrate on his lessons.

He needed to take advantage of this opportunity; there might not be another one, right? The hours passed and all he could think about was their meeting, the movie of what might happen playing a thousand times in his mind. He had to be genuine, interesting, safe and available.

All right, let's go for it!

When he reached the jetty, he threw down his backpack and opened the book he was reading. He eyes scanned the pages, but he wasn't taking anything in.

He waited, alone next to the sea. All he could hear were the seagulls screeching and mewling. He waited for hours, using his jacket to protect him from that grey cold, but no one came. Joana didn't show.

As he waited for her, he was once again struck by that feeling of sadness that plagued him whenever he thought of her. *There's something dark in her. Something that's shouting to get out.*

His mouth was dry with the anxiety of waiting. He drank water to relieve the salty tang that came from the vast expanse of crystalline blue liquid. The sea had always calmed him, especially at this time of day, when the sun was setting and it was starting to grow chillier.

He heard footsteps approaching. Samuel tried not to react, as if he were indifferent to her tardiness.

'Sorry, I lost track of time. Can I sit next to you?'

He said nothing. He looked up from the book on his lap and nodded. After a brief moment, Joana sat down, perturbed at his mysteriousness. Nothing else had piqued her attention until now, but he did. She didn't know whether it was because of the gentle movements with which he turned the pages of his book or the sweet aroma that hovered around him.

'It's called *A Thousand and One Sins*,' he said, with a slight smile on his face as he got up and stowed the book in his backpack. 'You seemed interested!'

'Thanks,' she said, unable to say anything else. The chill she felt in her belly was burning compared to the external temperature.

'What did you want to tell me?'

'I… nothing in particular. It's just that…' Joana fell silent and forced another smile. How could she tell him that she needed to be saved? To have someone to staunch her bleeding soul. How could she explain that he was her way out of this tangle of a life?

Samuel waited in silence. The balmy horizon extending at his feet, the soft warm sand and the song of the seabirds, the breaking waves and the bittersweet smell of the tide, almost made his whole body relax; the only tension was in his frowning forehead, which clearly conveyed his mood.

The evening was warm, while she was not. He looked at the horizon and said simply:

'That's where life begins.'

She got annoyed. She didn't want to hear philosophies – she couldn't deal with that just now. She needed him to notice her pain, to embrace her. But he couldn't see her falling.

'I'm fed up, you know that?' she interrupted. 'They say that life starts again every day. Tomorrow is a new day, that's fine, but what does that mean for those who aren't here any more?'

Then she got up.

'Speaking to you is like shouting in the dark. I whisper in the hope that you'll hear me…'

She turned round and started heading towards the beach, saying in a falsely animated tone: 'This was a bad idea. Everything's great. Forget I asked to talk to you. See you at school.'

And she walked away with a smile, as if everything was fine.

Except that that smile was the last one she could muster.

Oh Joana.
Everyone has secrets,
but some people don't have secrets so much as ruin.
And you are mine.

It was seven o'clock: the alarm went off and she got up hurriedly. It was the most important day of her life. Her last card to play. She was going to force herself to be happy – nothing else would work. She was going to walk to school with her spirit light, free from all guilt and anguish. For her, for her grandmother, for Samuel. Today was the day.

She walked down the street. It was her favourite one, old and different from all the others, the cobblestones reflecting the light, the ground slippery with morning dew, beds filled with tulips lining the way, dancing and perfuming the wind.

'Yes, yes! I can do this,' she thought, quickening her pace. 'This is the spirit. I'm going to convince myself that I'm happy.'

She took a deep breath, absorbing the world.

'I can just about see the puppies playing outside Mr Rui's caravan, even from this distance, and I can watch my grandmother's neighbours meeting on the café terrace, drinking their coffees, wearing hats to protect them from the sun, discussing the latest gossip. My grandmother isn't with them. She was like a mother to me, a lap to curl up in, the floor beneath my feet. I miss her so much. Every long second hurts, and just the idea of us is suffocating.'

On that street, dappled by the green of the trees and warmed by the yellow of the sun, she could hear the sea breeze.

It was summer, but the day had darkened.

Joana darkened too; she was living in winter again.

She lost control, seeing the neighbours in the café, so happy, so alive.

'Please, don't go...' she murmured, falling to her knees. 'I want more than just your memory, I want the moments.'

The day was lost. Not even the sight of Samuel, there on the street corner, watching her, made the slightest difference. She got up. She tried to force her legs to move, but it was useless.

She couldn't do it.

She grabbed on to the nearest tree, to be sure that it was still there and real. She couldn't breathe. Every attempt failed. Her vision was cloudy. At times, she didn't feel anything. The only sound she heard was her own heavy breathing. Then the memories hit her like a high-speed train, everything returning in the blink of an eye. The anger, the sadness, the regret, the hurt, the disappointment, the solitude, the panic: they all merged together to take up residence in her head. Whether she liked it or not, they weren't going away: they jostled for room inside her.

Joana ran off. Samuel watched her, concerned. The elderly neighbours at the cafe looked on, shocked to see her running towards the beach as she undressed, discarding her clothes and shoes as she ran.

She buried her feet in the cool morning sand. She ran to the sea and dived in impetuously.

She needed to feel alive. And quickly.

The cold water battered her body and, in some way, helped her relax. She lost herself, jumbled up in her own thoughts, the thoughts from which she could never escape.

He followed her. He brought spring with him. The lightness of cornfields waved in his hair. Hope shone in his green eyes. He approached across the sand.

'Take a deep breath...' he told her, standing at the waterline. 'It's all going to be fine.'

'Stop Samuel! Don't tell me what I want to hear. Pretty words won't do me any good now. There's no point coming with flowers after all the rusty nails I've been given along the way. Don't tell me what I want to hear , because I really don't want to break, and yet...'

He looked at her. She had a melodious voice that combined with the sweet, subtle aroma of her perfume, but she was racked with pain. Samuel took a deep breath, took off his shoes and entered the freezing sea.

He embraced her tightly.

'Whatever you want, you know you can count on me,' he murmured intensely.

She returned his gaze for a second and looked away. Silence fell. The waves murmured and bashed against their bodies, constant.

'You know... When I'm alone in the street, I confess my secrets to the moon, and hope that my grandmother hears them.'

He swallowed. He would have preferred a declaration of love. But he didn't speak – he wasn't going to ruin the moment. She maintained the silence for a while, before continuing.

'I can't remember a time when I wasn't constantly sad and suffocated by pain. I can't remember a time when a smile took no effort or a time when I didn't have to dress up as someone who's always happy for other people. Will that ever change? I just want to disappear.'

Samuel squeezed her arm.

'I'm here. I won't judge you. Tell me everything...'

'I can always hear her cries and feel her presence, I can't explain it. The good memories disappear and I'm just left with that... *that* day... Even now, after so much time, I still remember what happened that Friday as if it were yesterday... It was all my fault!'

The chill of the morning penetrated their bones, the waves lashed against their bodies, but neither seemed to feel it.

'It was an accident...' he exclaimed, firmly.

'It was no accident,' she interrupted furiously, amid salty tears. 'I remember every second, every detail. It was a cold winter night, the frost was forming quietly. I could hear our footsteps echoing along the street. Grandma's hands were trembling as she drew her coat around her weak body.'

She sobbed. Joana had never told anyone what happened. But now she had started, she couldn't stop.

'A man approached. He grabbed us. I shouted... I was the one who managed to escape that man's grasp and call the police. I left her behind... He was disgusting, he still is. By the time the police arrived, he had fled and she was on the ground... They said he was just a mugger, that her heart couldn't take it, but...'

'It wasn't your fault! You did exactly what you should have – you went to call for help.'

'I shouldn't have run away... leaving her there alone...'

Joana buried her face in Samuel's wet chest. 'I wanted her to live forever. I can't cope with how much I miss her. They say my sadness will end, or that's what they try to convince me. But she left and now the only season is winter.'

He grabbed her hand and slowly pulled her back to the beach. The sun was shining brightly, warming the fine sand. She managed to feel the summer breeze warming her soul.

'I can't do it, Samuel. I'm always in the dark, lost inside myself. I can't take any more. I have no family, no home… I don't even have myself, because I can't find myself. I'm so empty, so lost.'

Samuel sighed. The sound of seabirds calmed his mind as though it were a lullaby. He pushed the wet hair back from her face and looked intensely into her eyes. The time was now. He couldn't help her if he didn't give himself to her entirely.

He moved closer. Their lips touched, timidly at first, then tumultuously. He embraced her as if, in that closeness, he could mend her pain.

'Let me find you, Joana. Let me be your home.'

• • •

'Failed encounters' was commissioned by the young writers of Anselmo de Andrade Secondary School, Almada, Portugal: Bernardo Nobre, Eva Saraiva Pinho, Inês Gama, Isabella Baltazar, Madalena Rega, Margarida Correia, Ricardo Gil, Rita Patrício and Sofia Lopes.

Teachers: Rita Neves, Cristina Botelho, Vanda Cândido and Jorge Carvalho.

ABOUT THE AUTHOR

 **Maria Francisca Macedo** is a children's author. Her series *O Clube dos Cientistas (The Scientists' Club)*, combines adventures and experiments, and quickly became a success.

Her books are a reflection of her creativity and have been recognised by the Portuguese National Reading Plan and the CiênciaViva network of museums and centres. She is a member of the Editorial Committee of the magazine APEduC, on research and practices in the teaching of science, mathematics and technology.

She completed a post-graduate qualification in Children's Books in 2019, when she was also awarded the Maria Rosa Colaço prize for best unpublished children's work.

She currently writes, teaches and travels to schools from coast to coast, in meetings and workshops. When people ask what she does, she replies that she's a professional dreamer. And a nomad in her spare time!

Misunderstandings

Nuno Matos Valente

Translated from Portuguese by Beth Fowler

As soon as he got to class that morning, he saw her again. He sat down at the back, his usual place, and watched, never tiring of the soft lines of her face, the long hair, the air of someone who seemed attentive to everything without placing much importance on anything. She was sitting in the second row and chatting animatedly with a classmate.

João sat at an empty desk next to his friend.

'Hey, Ricardo, when are you going to tell her how you feel?'

He pretended not to understand.

'I think the teacher must be the only one who doesn't know you're smitten.'

His friend squirmed on his seat and didn't try to hide a smile.

'I'm going to talk to her today.'

'Seriously? Then what?'

'Then I'll tell you. Look, the teacher's speaking.'

Ricardo worked in a shoe shop after class and Rita worked in the shop across the street. The two of them usually left university at the same time, heading for Rua da Vitória, apparently indifferent to one another, despite always taking the same route.

In the middle of the afternoon, Rita would leave the shop to smoke standing by the door. Despite doing this regularly, and Ricardo having imagined dozens of ways to get into conversation with her, he lacked the courage. But that afternoon he had decided: he was going out to smoke too!

As soon as he saw Rita leaving the shop with her cigarettes, he followed suit. Of course, he couldn't avoid a coughing fit. But at least it had caught her attention from the other side of the street, and she unexpectedly crossed the road towards him.

'First time smoking, is it?' she mocked.

'No.'

'Then don't start. They say it kills!'

Before Ricardo had had time to think of a reply, she stubbed out the cigarette and returned to her job. The conversation hadn't gone exactly the way he had imagined it, but it was progress.

The rest of the week brought no developments: Rita didn't cross the street again, and she never looked behind her in class, so they had no more contact. Perhaps that tiny interaction, which had been the high point of his week, had meant nothing to her.

Saturday arrived. He got up late. He tried to study, get ahead on some essays, but he didn't really get anywhere with any of his tasks, interrupted by his constant checking of his mobile, social media, emails. He wondered how long this lethargy would last. Was this just the way he was now?

The clocks hadn't yet struck five when the first lights came on in the street, making little difference to the illumination of the neighbourhood other than producing a line of little dots that seemed to outline potential paths.

He sat still, pencil in hand hovering over a blank sheet, at a kitchen table strewn with crumpled papers.

When the streetlight outside his window came on too early, his hand started to move across the sheet and the point of his pencil started to release particles of graphite that formed, seventy-two times, the word Rita, Rita, Rita, Rita…

On the seventy-third repetition, he stopped and decided that the page should have the same destiny as the others that were piling scrunched up in front of him. He didn't complete the movement, though, as he was interrupted by a familiar buzzing from the smartphone on the chair next to him. The screen lit up with a nine-digit number he didn't recognise. The device vibrated a while longer until it finally fell silent. An icon showed the missed call. He threw all the pages in the bin and went to his bedroom, where he had decided to stare at his blank walls. The images occupying his mind were projected onto the wall: always the same subject, always the same images, always the same girl.

And there he sat for some time, until a seed of a thought, like a tiny hatching worm, started to bother him. First just a little speck, then a background noise and finally a fully-formed impulse transforming into electrical signals with which his brain would command the muscles of his hand and arm to move towards the telephone and the missed call icon that was still on the screen. He looked at the number but, despite his best efforts, he couldn't make any connection in his memory. He decided to return the call. He heard a beep, two beeps… and when he was about to disconnect, there was an answer from the other end.

'Hi, Ricardo?'

'Hello?'

'It's Rita.'

The sun was shining intensely that Sunday afternoon. Unable to control his desire to see her, he had arrived half an hour early in the park near work where they had arranged to meet.

Sitting on a wooden bench in front of a lake with ducks,

he watched the children playing around him. She arrived at the agreed time wearing a yellow dress.

Sitting side by side without talking, he jiggled his leg, agitated, while she, blushing, played with her hair.

'That girl over there on the slide could be me. Pigtails and everything.'

'You should go over and tell her that she'll be a beautiful woman when she grows up.'

They started meeting more frequently.

At university, they exchanged glances and kisses and words. As winter arrived, it got darker earlier and the city lights shone brightly as they reflected the wet ground.

One night, when the streets were very busy, they went out for dinner. In the restaurant where they met, the waiters had their hands full with all the orders, a detail of which the couple was blissfully unaware.

There is no word in the entire dictionary that could describe the perfection of the date. Nor the hours that followed; the days, and some weeks. They were the very definition of passion.

It wasn't unusual to see them holding hands on the street, making passers-by smile, whether because of the sweet memory it evoked or the confirmation that that harmony is indeed possible.

One Sunday afternoon they met in the park. Ricardo, sitting on a bench, saw his girlfriend approach with her dog, Feijão, on a lead.

'I was starting to get worried!'

'But I got here early…'

'Maybe I was just missing you.'

'I'll come even earlier tomorrow then.'

Feijão was running happily after the ducks as Rita and Ricardo tried to keep up with him without losing the thread of their conversation. When Feijão got tired he returned to his owner, who was finally able to sit down next to Ricardo on one of those silvery garden benches, under a large oak that offered some shade.

'Are you coming to watch my game tomorrow? My flat-mate invited you to lunch. His girlfriend is coming too. Ana, do you know her? Then we can go to your house.'

'Yes, of course, I'm taking Feijão to the vet, but after that I'll come to yours. Can I bring him?'

'That's fine. I know he doesn't bite.'

It was already growing dark when they finally decided to leave and said goodbye with a kiss. Ricardo made the long journey home walking on clouds. When he reached the door, he put his hand in his backpack to get the keys and felt a vibration: it was his mobile. He saw the name 'João' on the screen and, when he answered, heard a voice exclaim:

'Bro, you'll never guess what I've just seen!'

Ricardo hesitated as he unlocked the door, but risked asking: 'João? What's going on?!'

'I've just seen Rita go into my building. It looks like she's going to see my neighbour Fernando from second year!'

'Fernando? Which Fernando? Her ex?'

'Yuh-huh!'

Ricardo ended the call abruptly and, without looking back, headed for the building where his friend lived.

'Fernando,' he thought. 'Rita is still seeing him!'

When he was close to the building, he stopped and stood still, hidden in the dim light, like a wolf waiting for prey he doesn't really want to catch. Night was falling and the street was lit only by the moon, when finally Rita left that hateful building. She took a step forwards into the moonlight.

'Ricardo? What are you doing here?'

'I could ask you the same thing. I know all about it, Rita. Have you been cheating on me? How could you? After everything we've done for one another, I've shared my whole life with you and this is how you repay me? What does this guy have that I don't, Rita, hmm? Tell me! I want to know!'

'Ricardo! That's enough! Fernando and I are friends! You know something? If you don't trust me, then forget about me!'

'Rita!'

The girl was already moving away.

'Don't follow me!'

He should have run after her, tried to justify himself, but his feet refused to move.

He only came to his senses when he was back home. He sat on the sofa. He looked at the ceiling and took a deep breath in an attempt to calm down. After a few minutes, the feelings of anguish and rage started to dissipate and he plucked up the courage to call Rita. She didn't answer the first time. Or on the second attempt. Agitated, he paced from one side of the room to the other as he rehearsed a third attempt. At last Rita answered the call, but she remained silent.

'Hello? Rita? Can we talk calmly?!'

'Ricardo, I...' Rita started to say, interrupting him.

'Rita, please, don't say anything you might regret.'

'I need some time, I need some space, my head is all over the place. I think we should focus on ourselves for a while. Do you understand? Do you understand, Ricardo? Hello? Hello?'

He decided to respect Rita and give her the time she had asked for. For that reason, when he passed her at university he only said hello and asked how she was, to which Rita responded that she was fine and returned the question. Time passed and their relationship was limited to that. Until one day she decided to seek him out to talk.

Ricardo was in the corridor, outside the room where he usually had classes. He was facing the door Rita had entered and was laughing at something João had said. She was watching him intently from afar and, when their eyes finally met, she didn't know how to interpret that look.

She walked hesitantly towards him. She could feel Ricardo's gaze on her as she moved slowly, thinking about what to say. When she had almost reached them, João moved off – he must have known there was a delicate conversation coming, one that didn't need spectators.

'Hi...' she said timidly, finally confronting him, face to

face after so much time being practically strangers.

'Hi… Rita, how's it going?' he replied, unsure of what to say.

'Look, Ricardo… I don't want to beat around the bush. We both know why I'm here and I don't think there's any point pretending that everything's all right when it isn't. We're both adults and I know that it seems a bit hypocritical to say this after I've been the one to avoid this conversation, but I really needed some time to think about us… if there is still an us…' she added in a low voice.

'Rita, I respected your space. I gave you time to think and I also made the most of that time to do some thinking myself and you know I love you. I think we should give this another try. I really believe our relationship is much more than this. I jumped to conclusions, I know. But when I saw you with him…'

'Ricardo, love is fundamental in a relationship, but it also has to be based on trust, on respect. How could you think I was cheating on you? From the moment you get involved with someone you have to get it into your head that all your choices, your attitudes, don't just affect you. You hurt me: you showed me that you don't trust me, and you don't trust in the strength of our love, our intimacy. How do you expect me to continue in a relationship where my partner doesn't trust me? Where my boyfriend follows me, tries to control me?'

'Rita, listen, I know I made a mistake but…'

She raised her hand, as if asking him to wait and continued:

'When I say that, I'm not placing all the blame on you. You weren't the only one in the relationship... I have my share of blame too, I should have been honest with you from the start and... looking back now, I don't know why I wasn't. But it's done now and we have to deal with the consequences. Perhaps what happened was just a good excuse to put an end to this...'

'You still don't get it, do you? I don't want to put an end to this. I want to fight for us, I want to fight for you, Rita!'

'There's nothing left to fight for, Ricardo!' she said, as a solitary tear ran down her right cheek. 'The sooner we finish this the better. For the sake of all we've been through, I'm begging you not to make it more complicated than it already is.'

Ricardo accepted Rita's decision, but in his heart he felt an immense rage, an inexplicable resentment.

Days passed and Ricardo couldn't come to terms with it. So he decided to follow her again. It was the worst decision he could have made, he knew, but sometimes there's something inside us we can't control.

He followed her again and again, countless times, and she never noticed a thing. Until one day. It seemed to him that she was heading for the library closest to her house, perhaps to avoid seeing him in the university library, but it turned out to be rather more sinister than that. A boy? Was that a boy?!

He couldn't believe his eyes! Was that Fernando?

He approached her.

'Well well, Rita! I was right not to trust you after all!'

'Ricardo?!' she blurted out, standing up. 'What are you doing here? Were you spying on me? Again?'

'And for good reason, it would seem!'

Fernando was visibly embarrassed and didn't say a word.

'I can't believe that after all we've been through because of your jealousy, you're still following me! And the worst thing is that we aren't even going out any more! We aren't together, Ricardo. Could you get that into your head once and for all? It was really hard, but I finished with you precisely because there was no trust. The least you could have done was give me a bit of peace!'

'Listen,' said Fernando, moving closer. 'She's already told you to leave her in peace! Or don't you understand simple language?'

Blinded by hatred, he only came to his senses when Fernando fell down, the result of a punch that neither of them had time to avoid. He dropped to the floor, hit his head and fell unconscious.

'Fernando! Ricardo, what have you done? Fernando? Someone call an ambulance! Call 112! Hurry!'

The ambulance arrived and took Fernando to hospital. Rita went in the ambulance with the injured boy and, as the paramedic closed the door, she threw him a final glance, one that Ricardo couldn't decipher.

He called an Uber and made his way to the hospital behind them.

'Excuse me. A boy called Fernando Lopes has just been admitted. It can't have been more than half an hour ago, he came by ambulance. Do you know where he is?'

The receptionist consulted the computer and wrote a few words on a piece of paper, which she handed to him.

'This is the floor, bed 233. You can go up in that lift.'

He entered the lift, went up to the second floor and headed for the ward. He trembled when he saw the name of the department: Oncology.

He walked in, feeling a chill in his stomach as if his heart was freezing with every step he took in that dark, solitary passageway. Before he went much further in, he saw Rita ahead of him, sitting with her head between her hands like a Greek goddess in tears, adorning the end of that sad corridor.

'Ricardo? Again? Can't you leave me in peace?'

'Wait, Rita! I came to say sorry! Seriously. I want to see Fernando and ask his forgiveness, I feel so terrible about it!'

'Fernando is in there, but we can't go in.'

'Why not? And why is he on this floor?'

'He was recently diagnosed with a brain tumour and I was the only one he told – not even his own parents know! That's why they brought him right here!

'So that's why you…'

'Yes! I didn't tell you because he asked me not to. What did you want, for me to abandon him at this stage? Because of your jealousy?'

149

'There's no way I could have known.'

'It would be best if you leave. He can't see you now and I… I don't want to see you.'

The alarm went off. He opened one eye, looked at the clock:

7:20

'I have class. But I don't feel like getting up at all,' he thought.

The alarm beeped again. He had nodded off.

7:29.

'It's so early. I wonder how Fernando is? And Rita? Will she be with him?'

The alarm was persistent:

7:36

His face was heavy on the warm pillow, the weight of his body sweetly misshaping the mattress.

'Rita, I hope you can forgive me. Can you hear me, Rita? Are you there somewhere? I know you'll forgive me. I don't know what came over me, I'm sorry, I'm sorry!'

7:45. 7:54. 8:03

'I'm not going to class, Rita. I need to rest. I'm glad you came back. You're different.'

'Rest, my love. Everything's going to be fine.'

'Do you forgive me?'

'Of course, Ricardo. Love forgives everything. You know that what we have is love, don't you?'

8:12

'Will you stay with me?'
'Of course, my love. Forever. Here, with you.'

8:21

8:30

8:39

...

• • •

'Misunderstandings' was commissioned by Class 11°7 of the course Scientific-Humanistic Languages and Humanities of the Secondary School Fernão Mendes Pinto, Almada, Portugal: Alexandre Abrantes da Silva, Andreia Filipa Pedreira Pinto, Beatriz Filipa Ramalho Abreu, Beatriz Gomes Rebelo, Beatriz Silva Santos, Carlos Miguel Mota Dinis, Daniel Alexandre Gonçalves Ucuahamba, Daniela André Gunza, Daniela Filipa dos Santos Simões, Elisiane Euridice Ramos Tavares, Emanuelle Lorena Basilio de Oliveira, Erica Martins de Borba, Ines Figueira Correia, João Filipe Babo de Almeida Félix, Leonardo Filipe Nascimento Pedroso, Luis Carlos Pestana Pica, Luís Henrique Mourato Rosinha, Mafalda Nabais Baldo Figueiredo Bóia, Mariana Pinto Correia Piedade Barros, Nadine Simone Silva Monteiro, Rafaela Ferreira Esteves, Rodrigo de Oliveira Figueiredo Tito, Rúbia de Fátima Carvalho Marques da Costa and Tomas Fernandes Santos.

Teacher: Sandra Videira

ABOUT THE AUTHOR

Nuno Matos Valente was born in Lisbon and grew up in the town of Castelo Branco, where he moved in 1980. He has lived in Alcobaça since 2007. He teaches Visual Education and is an editor for Edições Escafandro.

He is co-author of the *Segredos (Secrets)* collection of school textbooks for the first phase of primary education, published by Raiz Editora.

He is the author of the young adult fiction collection *A Ordem do Poço do Inferno* (*The Order of the Pit of Hell*), recommended by the Portuguese National Reading Plan.

He was a leading figure in the study and compilation of traditional creatures in the popular Portuguese imagination, which resulted in the publication of the first *Bestiário Tradicional Português (Traditional Portuguese Bestiary)*, published by Escafandro in 2016.

In 2019, he was awarded a literary creation grant by the Directorate General for Books, Archives and Libraries.

Chorus

Inês Barata Raposo

Translated from Portuguese by Beth Fowler

The first thing you need to know about us is that it doesn't matter who we are. These are our stories; in a parallel universe, they could be yours. Some days it reassures us to know that we are all secondary characters on the stage of humanity. On others, we feel as though the planet's centre of gravity is set right in between our shoulders. If we were butterflies, we would think twice before each beat of our wings.

We resent philosophy, which only presents us with questions. We crush arguments and dismantle determinisms. We have our doubts about literature, about songs of friendship and romantic love, whose red is either passion or blood. In our world, red is more likely to be the colour of Benfica, of ketchup or merely a primary colour. We're fine about not knowing who we are, where we're going or what we're doing here. We know there's no cheat sheet to solve the mathematics of time. Yesterday we were the dream of a tiny ant; today we are humans; tomorrow is a blank page.

TAKE 1

I avoid talking about myself, sharing feelings and their consequences. In my neighbourhood, we learn the value of information at an early age. Much of what I know I would rather not know: who was at the neighbours' house until what time, where the men go after dinner, what the women say while they're waiting for them. And then there's everything I don't know, which I pay the price for whenever I let myself get carried away by illusions: what became of my father? Will my little brother respect me when he grows up? Can we choose our own aunties and love them like a mother? These aren't things you talk about, but I suspect there are others like me, constantly juggling between answers we can't give and questions we can't ask.

Apart from music, I don't tend to identify with the version of the world they want to serve up. Whenever I'm stuck for words, I grab onto bars of music. I like the idea that a bar is to rap more or less what a verse is to a sonnet. I find it fitting, in a flawed kind of way.

I grew up in a 'hood
Where patience
Did no good
Half-truths ran
Alongside our childhood
But then the silence
Swallowed all it could

I've even selected the soundtrack for the walk. Today there's no pretension, bling or flirtation when I connect my headphones. After a morning of sleep-inducing classes about lives and times that mean nothing to me, I'm going to take control and listen to something that makes me think this guy knows what he's talking about, he could be one of my brothers, one of the people I see every day on my street. The first artist happens to be a man who cries in secret, who knows about 'kids inside,' a lack of food on his plate, crime in the neighbourhood. But his family also taught him the importance of having principles, of letting go of hate and resentment, of believing in a more beautiful world. All this in three and a half minutes: it's more therapeutic than three weeks trying to exchange a few words with Mum between her extra shifts and trips to the supermarket. I hurry down the stairs and knock on the door of Mena, the matriarch of the whole neighbourhood.

In the kitchen, on the lower floor, there are benches that always have room for one more, two more, or all comers. On days I manage to catch her alone, she tells me about her children who left the neighbourhood, far removed from the bad life, the scams. Now they're part of the system, she says proudly to other mothers, like someone saying that there's always hope. I've never met them, as they're older than me, but Mena assures me we'd get on well. Apparently we all have our heart in the right place – on the left, 'just like the revolution that brought us here.' It's a typical game of Mena's: to make some mysterious utterance which leaves us with only two options: pretend we know what she's talking about, which is risky as we can't continue the conversation, or ask her to tell us in more detail, which always results in epic stories that cross the Atlantic. Gradually I'm starting to understand this way of forcing us to converse without asking questions. In the neighbourhood, being a mother to all isn't for everyone. That's why I find it hard when my friends confess their truths in public, in class or on social media.

For the last few weeks, the whole school has fallen under the spell of an unknown figure, someone who shares everything about their dream lifestyle in HD: the fridge full to the brim, brand-new clothes, a view of the park, a lawned garden. Today the big existential doubt haunting this person is a question of style: 'Dear followers, help me! I don't know which jacket to wear.' They use motivational hashtags, want us believe that being vulnerable is a superpower, never a weakness. I'd say it's neither of those things: vulnerability is a privilege that varies depending on your postcode. In a world where windows have bars and roofs are lookout posts, I was pretty much born to hold a bucket and trowel in my hand, ready to build the invisible walls that protect me. If there are windows, I'll place them high up so that no one can see out. The door is hidden and reserved for family alone: not the family that shares my blood but the one that bleeds alongside me day by day. One day I'll have to leave, test those voices that tell me 'come here' and show them that I can go without forgetting where I came from. Mena's sons say they want to repay the neighbourhood for everything it gave them, just as soon as they get that deal, that opportunity, that fortune. I don't know them, but if they came here more often I'd put an idea in their heads, like androids when they learn the subtleties of human nature: instead of repaying everything, just repay the good stuff. That's my plan, for one day. But today is Wednesday, my mobile battery is low, and I have to hurry if I want to get home with music still in my ears. Tomorrow, it will be a different playlist.

TAKE 2

'Black jacket or yellow windbreaker?' Helping an influencers choose their clothes for the day gives me a feeling of control which I've been lacking recently. After checking Twitter and exercising my right to vote on behalf of a black jacket, I choose the list of songs for my return home. I have a free afternoon and, if I pedal at a good pace, I'll get there before everyone else. More than wanting to be alone, I find myself wanting to go back in time, before the shock of lost love rocked the foundations of my family. The soundtrack for my journey home is filled with songs from my childhood – I listen to them in private mode, of course. Nostalgia is a luxury that adolescence still won't allow. I'll only be able to revisit the Disney hits when I hit my mid-twenties crisis, and even then only ironically. That is, when I become a serious person in society, with a job and a family, then the popular culture of the 2000s will be my banner – my way of saying to the world that once upon a time I was young and had interests beyond checking my bank balance. I move along the cycle path like a wrecking ball.

Sometimes you need to knock something down to build it again. Every time there's a row at home and my little sister complains to our grandmother, my parents' marriage turns into a civil construction site. Using her trite metaphors, Gran would have us believe that the foundations were never very firm anyway, that the project wasn't well planned, that certain main-beams were discovered too late, that the walls started to crack early on, and that it's desperately in need of a bridge to join the two sides. There's undeniably a risk of collapse.

For the sake of my mental health, I avoid getting involved in that conversation. But I do have an alternative to my grandmother's theory: the marriage fell apart so slowly that no one noticed, the floor opened up and devoured the rubble; there was zero left to build it up again. It's impossible to criticise my little sister for believing in happy endings, despite my crazy urge to tell her what I know about our parents. I take a deep breath, straighten the handlebars and skip to the next song.

'Some things you can't tell your sister 'cause she's still too young,' sings James TW. Amen to Our Lady of the Random Order of the Holy Church of All-Powerful Spotify. Today the algorithm is on my side.

After several panic attacks and just as many therapy sessions, I made my peace with the fact that I'm living in the wreckage of a marriage. That reality became clear when I noticed the kind of body language Lopes's parents use. We were doing a group activity and at lunchtime we met our friend's parents, sitting on a bench. The two of them were humming as they alternated lettuce leaves and slices of ham on our sandwiches. Out of nowhere, Mr Lopes rested his hand lightly on Mrs Lopes's shoulder, followed by what I can only describe as a gentle nudge, like a cat, head against head, pure tenderness. At first, I felt like vomiting with rage. The envy of seeing that the Lopes family lived in a house with a robust floor, walls and roof. Oh well. The waves of sadness are there to be surfed, not to drown ourselves or our friends in them. It wasn't Mr and Mrs Lopes's fault.

I never saw my parents holding hands, kissing or exchanging those caresses that embarrass everyone else around. I saw hands snatched back at the last second, various sad embraces and the kind of slaps that echo on the other person's cheek.

The arguments, to tell the truth, are less and less frequent. Just as the gestures disappeared, the words, too, ran out. If I survived the terror of the trenches – plates flying across the room, like in the movies – there's no reason for me to be a casualty of the Cold War. I live with two ghost-adults, who give me lodging, free internet and an unlimited supple of Lidl frozen lasagnes. I play my hand of cards and practise the art of strategic withdrawals. The modus operandi is simple: do the housework, help with jobs and don't make waves. That way I avoid the front line of battle.

Wednesdays, like today, are easy. I have lunch at school, I pedal full speed, and for two hours I have the castle to myself. I lose myself looking at our faces in the dusty frames. Sometimes I flick through the family album forgotten on the coffee table. I go to their room – which to be honest is Mum's room; my dad barely sleeps at home – and I open the wardrobe. I take out one of my mother's summer dresses and my dad's interview suit, and I lay them out one on each side of the bed and I lie down in the middle. I pretend that the ceiling light is an old-fashioned camera, I pull the sleeves of the vacant clothes closer to me and I smile. *Click*. We're a happy family again.

TAKE 3

'For people who know what they want.' As if it's that easy. As if anyone knows. I don't know why I keep looking for signs in adverts on the metro. Don't these people understand that life is more than a parade of choices? I bury myself in my mobile on the way home, while online

I have people to help me with the most innocuous decisions. It's a relief when my followers choose the clothes I wear – it's one less decision to make. The deep waters of identity are so difficult to navigate that I grab on to what I have: questions, looks of the day, make-up tutorials, motivational phrases and articles about gender identity. All wrapped up in the beautiful package of social networks, in a perfectly curated profile, with no hint of the double life I lead, the *digital me* laughing in the face of the *real me*.

This morning as I tried on the black jacket, the winner in the last vote on the blog, I didn't recognise myself in the mirror. I know that sounds serious, but I don't think there's any great cause for alarm. I've often felt like this, like a strip of toothpaste on the end of the brush. It isn't just blue, or red, or white. But it always has those three colours. And to make things worse, after a few scrubs and gargles, it ends up as a pinkish foam with no trace of the original colours. Could that be the true nature of the toothpaste or does it end up like that purely from having been lathered up during brushing? Naturally this has very little to do with oral hygiene and everything to do with what Aunt Salete tends to call 'the usual quandaries of adolescence' in whispered phone conversations with my mother. Both consider themselves queens of discretion, but the interrogations they subject me to during family lunches are not remotely innocent. Sometimes they ask me about my favourite actors and actresses – they want to know which poster would fit best on my bedroom wall. They try to grab on to what they have, any clue that allows them to peek into the box of tangled cables and buttons that is my head. Other times, the questions are so dull that I can barely tell whether they're part of some grand plan. 'That colour suits your sister, don't you think?' or 'So, how are Benfica doing this season?' I still have a lot to learn about the methods of emotional espionage passed down from generation to generation.

The day started off calmly enough; the jacket selected for me was lightweight. I survived a morning of classes and a test. I caught the metro in enough time to get a window seat – it's a long journey home. Still, the advert caught me by surprise. 'People who know what they want.' Seriously? Message to the Cosmos: if this is the kind of sign you're going to send, you'd be better off keeping quiet. It's the old story of which box we want to put ourselves in, this time in A3 format with an unmissable credit plan. On one side of the poster, a smiling woman with red lipstick and high heels; on the other, a confident man in a full suit and gold watch. It's this or that, for girls or for boys. The advert reduces life to a never-ending ice cream counter from which we can only choose two flavours. Strawberry or vanilla, no mixing, and it's forever. Anyone who wants a sample of another flavour has to stretch out their transparent plastic spoon and justify themselves in front of the jury of good manners. Even if they don't want any of the flavours, or perhaps two at the same time, or they think there are more ways of enjoying ice cream than a cup or a cone. And yes, I admit, I waver between distrusting people who know what they want and wanting to be one of them. It's a conversation I need to have with my parents, but I've found it hard to pluck up the courage. If only there was a way of knowing that speaking to them was the path that Fate wanted me to follow...

Okay, I admit that's why, without meaning to, I find myself looking for a sign on the way home, with only one certainty: I need to speak to someone in flesh and blood, disconnect from confessional tweets and my followers' support. The only way to feel at home in my own skin is to open the box where I keep my fear of exposing myself. The metro fills up. A girl of around my age grips on to the rail. She has a duffel bag in all the colours of the rainbow. This could be my sign – I'm alert to anything. I start to outline a plan for when I get home. The most important thing is not to connect to the internet, and have zero distraction until I've spoken to them.

I enter the house and connect to the net. How to make a plan fail in the warm-up phase. I have a private message:

> *@lov4bites, you don't know me, but I want you to know that I've been following you for a long time and I admire your courage to be yourself. You've helped me a lot with facing problems at home. Keep spreading the magic. Thankz!*

The sign took its time, but it arrived. Finally I know what to do. I make my Twitter account public and send the WhatsApp link to my parents. I hear the *ping* of the notification in the living room and I turn to stone. I see the two ticks go from grey to blue. Several minutes pass; no one replies. Then Mum and Dad come into the kitchen, crush me in their embrace and cry a little. I cry too, but not just a little. Then we laugh like crazy until we're exhausted. The weight is lifted. I still have my uncertainties, but this time I'm the one who tells them it's going to be all right.

• • •

'Chorus' was commissioned by the young writers of Cacilhas Tejo Secondary School, Portugal.

ABOUT THE AUTHOR

 **Inês Barata Raposo** was born in Castelo Branco, Portugal. She won the Branquinho da Fonseca Expresso/ Gulbenkian and Tábula Rasa 2019 prizes with the young adult book *Coisas que Acontecem* (*Things that Happen*), published by Bruaá in 2018, which is recommended by the Portuguese National Reading Plan and included in the 'White Ravens' catalogue of the International Youth Library.

She was shortlisted for the literature category of the national Young Creators competition in 2018. She has had stories published in various anthologies.

She lives in a village in the interior of Portugal and works as an advertising copywriter.

The Little, Big Love

Eldrid Johansen

Translated from Norwegian by Nancy Langfeldt

The sound of my alarm clock cuts through the air. I take off like a rocket, realising in that moment that I've been sat waiting right on the very edge of the sofa. My heart is hammering in time with my steps, which are clattering over the parquet floor toward the hallway. I screech to a halt in front of the wardrobe mirror and run my hands through my newly-washed hair. I brushed it just a minute ago. More than twenty strokes with my hairbrush. Even though brushing the knots that form at the nape of my neck, where the curls and straight hair tangle together, is one of my least favourite things to do. Luckily my hair still has a glossy shine to it and is hanging straight down my back. I smile a little encouraging smile at the eyes gleaming back at me from the mirror: *You can do this! You look good and are well-prepared.*

So I tug the door open. I can feel my cheeks catching fire, and I guarantee they are lit up now, Christmas red. Just in time to meet the wonky smile that makes my body explode. A wild prickling on my skin spreads like a pandemic via my shuddering heart, all the way down till it's tickling the soles of my feet.

'Hi,' I say. My voice sounds tinny and strangely unfamiliar. I hurry back down the hallway. For goodness' sake. Have I lost the ability to speak properly? I clear my throat. Try again. 'Come in!'

'Thank you,' he says, closing the door behind him.

I watch as he kicks off his chalk-white trainers. In one smooth motion he takes off his black leather jacket and hangs it on the hook I have just cleared.

Something bubbles up at the back of my throat. One arm of my pink waterproof jacket, the one I removed from his hook and stuffed under a pile, is sticking out.

'Are you hungry?' I ask. I'm now looking away to try and regain control over my voice. 'We have pizza and salad.'

'That would be great,' he says. 'Are you on your own?'

On my own. If only I was.

'Only Kim's here,' I say. 'He's watching Netflix in the living room.'

I turn towards him again. My brain is yelling at my cheeks to stop burning, but I'm not sure my cheeks are getting the message, or can be bothered to do anything about it. 'The food's all ready.'

He nods. Smiles again. The wonderful smile that makes my heart skip a beat. Not to mention the smouldering blue gaze that sets off a wild dance party in my stomach every time my eyes meet his. On the way to the kitchen I become very aware of my steps. Does he think I walk weird? Badly? Too fast? The whole time I can feel him right behind me. It's so strange: even though I haven't heard a peep out of him, I can tell he's there. It's like my senses are turned up to the max when he's near. I noticed it last time too. I become as sensitive as Star, Grandad's golden retriever, who knows when I'm coming and waits, tail wagging and ready, long before the door opens.

'Help yourself,' I say, pointing towards the kitchen counter.

While I scan my brain for what to say, I watch him load up his plate. I wonder at how holding a plate and filling it with slices of pizza and salad can be done so elegantly. His face is as beautiful as a film star on a poster. His body too. Everything about him is perfect. Before I met him, I didn't know that actual boys could look like this in real life. Or that a boy's hair could so perfectly frame a face in messy waves.

He looks up from his plate. It's like he's studying me, before he asks, 'Would you like some too?'

I feel myself lift my shoulders up to my ears. I try and look like it's no big deal.

'Maybe I'll have a little slice,' I say. 'I've already eaten, but I could have a tiny bit more.'

He smiles.

'I'd rather not eat alone.'

I serve myself and sink down into the chair right across from him at the kitchen table. How hard it is to find words. Normally I'm a chatterbox. Now it feels like all sentences have crept away to hide in the inner realms of my brain. They are elusive and impossible to trap.

After a period of silent chewing, he looks at me.

'Do you maybe want to watch a film? After we've eaten?'

I shake inwardly. I nod. Cast my eyes down. This is what I have dreamt about and looked forward to the most. Him and me. On the sofa. Alone.

'Do you have anything in mind?' he continues. 'Any films, that is?'

Of course I do. The piece of paper with the list on it is still under my pillow, though I memorised my film suggestions ages ago. Earlier today I thought I had covered everything, but have I? I don't want to make the wrong choice. He must absolutely not get bored or get the wrong idea about me.

'There are lots of films I'd like to watch.' I swallow. 'Series too. What about you?'

He looks up.

'I'll watch anything, me.'

Anything? A shudder I really hope he doesn't notice races through me.

'Kim…' I clear my throat. 'He has to go to bed first.'

'Sure,' he says and pulls his phone out of his pocket. For far too long he sits and scrolls.

When he finally gets up, putting his plate in the sink and heading for the living room, I follow. It's happening! Finally!

'Hi mate,' he says, ruffling Kim's hair. 'How's it going?'

Kim nods, his eyes glued to the TV screen.

'Are you watching anything good?' Kim nods again. Instead of switching it off, he settles down next to Kim on the sofa. Irritation grows in me. The clock is ticking. Are they going to sit there and watch a stupid, noisy cartoon? Doesn't he understand that every minute with Kim is eating into my time? Into *our* time.

My heart beats faster and faster as I turn and stomp back into the kitchen. I steady myself against the counter by the sink. Seriously! We don't have time for this. Before we know it she'll be back and then it will be too late. I turn on the tap and let the water splash over the greasy plates. When they are both thoroughly rinsed, I go back to the living room.

'Bedtime, Kim,' I say.

'What? Can't I watch the end?'

'It's too late,' I continue. 'You can watch the rest tomorrow.'

'You're so strict,' whines Kim. 'Don't you think she's too strict?'

'She's right,' he says. His laughter waves towards me.

So soft and warm, it ripples deep in me. 'Tomorrow is another day.'

With a sigh, Kim gets up off the sofa and disappears towards the bathroom. I've already laid out his pyjamas and toothbrush. I've even loaded up the toothpaste. How I'm going to get hold of the Lego set I promised in return for him brushing his own teeth and going to bed without a song or a story, I'll figure out tomorrow.

'Wow. That's great,' he says when Kim disappears. 'It's so good that Kim can sort himself out these days.'

Once more he pulls his phone out of his trouser pocket, eyes fixed on the screen. I wait until I can hear Kim has finished in the bathroom and the bedroom door clicks shut. Nice. The first part of the plan has been a success. Now it's my turn.

Not until I've plopped down next to him does he look up from his phone. I notice that he turns the screen away from me. He's so preoccupied with his phone. He's not been like this before. I feel a painful pressure in my chest. Is he texting someone? A girl? I pull the blanket that Kim has just been using over me. It's still warm.

'Film night!' I say, in a voice that even I can tell is much too high-pitched. He puts his phone on the table like it's a commando manoeuvre.

'Let's do this' he says.

I pick up the remote again and find my number one film choice, *Love Actually*. The most romantic comedy of all time, apparently. There's no way back now.

He doesn't say anything, so I click the film on and lean back into the sofa, as relaxed as I can be when he's sitting this near me. When the intro, full of kisses and cuddles and joyful reunions at an airport, is over, I gasp for air and realise I have been holding my breath. He gives me a look, smiles briefly and leans back too.

'Are you sure you're ok with this film?'

'I'm ok with it,' I nod.

A washed-up popstar is singing in a music studio. People are getting ready for Christmas. I can forget about following all the details of these various stories. Instead I use my energy to inch closer and closer. At last I'm right up against him. When the warmth of his thigh flows into mine, I can't stop trembling. He looks at me. This time with raised eyebrows.

'Are you cold?'

I shrug my shoulders, wrap the blanket round me and curl up. 'Maybe a little.'

'Come here,' he says, putting an arm around my shoulder. 'I'll warm you up.'

If he could have seen the look on my face. If he'd known how my insides were burning. Seen the goose pimples appearing. As he pulls me close, I have to really concentrate on remembering to breathe. It's not just his warmth. His smell is almost too much for me. A whiff of boy, clean hair and cologne. Soon I have sunk completely into the crook of his arm and slowly my breathing calms down. Sitting together, side by side under the blanket, it's like our bodies melt together into a single breathing organism.

I close my eyes. If only this feeling could be stored in my body and brain. If only this moment could last forever. This is where I want to be. Now and forever.

I jump when the porch door opens. Next she's standing in the living room doorway. She's still wearing her coat and boots.

'What a cosy scene,' she smiles. 'Has everything been alright?'

I lean heavily – insistently – hard against him, at the same time as I turn my face and look up. *Stay. Stay here with me.* But instead of obeying my thoughts, he pushes me tenderly aside, grabs his phone, stands up and leaves me under the blanket, alone.

'It's been great,' he says and moves towards Mamma. 'Kim is asleep and we've watched a film.'

As he approaches, Mamma opens her bag and pulls out her wallet.

'Thank you so much,' she smiles as she hands him the notes. 'The children clearly love you. You really are a dream babysitter!'

• • •

'The Little, Big Love' was commissioned by students from the upper secondary schools of Haugaland, Kopervik, Skeisvang and Vardafjell in Norway.

ABOUT THE AUTHOR

 **Eldrid Johansen** (1973) has published many books for children and young people since her debut, *Sara wants to be a star,* in 2005. In addition to writing books, Eldrid works as singer and producer of literature in the Government school program The Cultural Rucksack. For many years she has also arranged workshops in creative writing around the country. She also speaks about her books and gives special concerts and performances for children. She has visited literature festivals, libraries and schools and is a popular performer.

Her book *Write brilliantly!* was nominated for the Brage Award and won the Department of Culture's prize for best factual book for children and young people in 2016. In 2017 *The Pharaoh's Curse* was nominated for ARK's children's book prize. Her twenty-fifth book, *From you saw me,* a novel for young adults, was published in August 2020.

The Bet

Annette Münch

Translated from Norwegian by Nancy Langfeldt

Sunday 1st February

Selma scratches her close-shaven neck. Behind her the February rain trickles down the window. I imagine that the sky is crying at how pathetic we are: three hours on a sticky leather sofa at the back of a café…

'Hurry!' I say. 'My bladder is about to burst and I feel sick from all the cinnamon swirls…'

All the other customers have left the building. The guy in the speakers is rapping for Selma, me, and the empty plastic cups on the table in front of us. At the other end of the café a boy with a green apron is wiping the counters with a cloth. He moves an advert for a 'Two for one on Valentine's day' offer.

'Do you know what would make the perfect Valentine's day?' asks Selma, drumming her neon-green finger nails on the table top.

'You're delaying again. Go and talk to him!' I sigh and sink back in to the sofa. 'Anyway, Valentine's day is stupid. No one really cares.'

Selma picks the straw out of one of the plastic cups and starts chewing its end.

'A trip to Rome,' she continues, ogling like she's undressing the boy with her gaze. 'Eating pepperoni pizza at a table with a red checked tablecloth. And hiring a Vespa to cruise through town. So romantic!'

'You are in fact the only one person I know who cares about Valentine's day,' I say, stifling a yawn. 'It's not a big deal. Last year I spent the day watching Ulrik play Fortnite. The year before I waited for Marcus in a shopping centre for two hours – he'd forgotten we had a date.'

At last Selma tears her eyes away from the boy behind the counter. She takes the straw out of her mouth and sticks it into her black side bun.

'You're just spoiled. You've always had a boyfriend on Valentine's day! Isn't this the first time you've been single?'

I shrug my shoulders. Selma doesn't understand how tiring it can be to have a boyfriend. Insecurity, stupid misunderstandings, the fear of getting dumped. I turn and study the photos on the wall. They are all taken from the air. It's easy to recognise the pine forest around the town, with dark bathing pools and narrow foot-paths criss-crossing like a nervous system through the landscape. According to the caption underneath, the photographer is called Leon Knutson.

'This time I'm staying single for a long time,' I mumble.

'You are never single for long. I bet you'll get with-drawal symptoms after two weeks without compliments and reassurance about how pretty and smart you are.'

Selma grins as she smears hot pink lip gloss across her mouth.

'If you stop being so rude, maybe you'll get a boyfriend yourself one day,' I answer.

'At least I'm not afraid of being alone! You are. That's why you go out with childish, self-obsessed guys who sit around gaming on Valentine's day.'

'No one takes that day seriously!'

Selma leans back on her chair, thoughtful, and slowly twists the piercings in her ears.

'I bet you won't manage to stay single until 14th February,' she says, after a few seconds of silence.

'Of course I can manage that!'

'Fine! Loser has to wear a bra on their head for a whole day.'

I shake my head. 'So childish.'

'Exactly, so it's doubly embarrassing. People will definitely film you.'

'Film *you*,' I correct her and grab Selma's hand.

'Choose a lacy one,' she whispers. 'To match your curls.'

I can't help smiling. Just then the Town Hall clock rings

out over the street. It's eight o'clock. The boy removes muffins and filled bagels from the glass display case. I lean across the table towards Selma.

'Listen, this is lame. You are about to lose your job because you have swapped too many shifts, just so you can sit here and stare at him. You drink coffee, which you don't like. And he doesn't even know your name…'

Selma rotates one of the plastic cups towards me. Her name is written in block capitals with a black felt tip pen.

'Over the last few weeks I've bought eighteen drinks off him, and got two for free,' she smirks, smugly. 'I think he knows my name.'

'So go and speak to him before he reports you for *stalking*! The café is closing,' I command. I put my hand on hers and add more mildly, 'You are the coolest person I know. You can do this. Just take the straw out of your hair first.'

Selma can climb up cliff sides, speaks up in a group and can lock herself in a bedroom and strip for some guy at a party. But the moment she stops at the counter a ruby red colour rises up her neck. Her thin fingers escape into her hoodie pockets. The boy comes over, drying his hands on a towel and explaining that service is unfortunately over.

Selma answers haltingly. She's talking too fast, too loud. I want to hide my face in the sofa cushions. My best friend is a shit-hot dancer, makes people laugh and can talk her way out of all imaginable scenarios, but she is terrible at being in love.

'I got a tattoo yesterday! Do you want to see?' she squeaks, thrusting her right arm across the counter. 'A tattoo artist I know did it after they closed up.'

Before the boy can answer she raises her arm and shows off the cursive writing on her light pink skin. 'Forza! It's Italian and means 'go' or 'you can do it'. Or 'strength'. I love Italy. My dad is Italian. Or was. I mean he's not dead. I don't think.'

I groan inwardly, grab my leather bag and stand up. This is an emergency situation.

'Come on Selma! Lilly's been dumped, we have to hurry!'

I throw my arm around her shoulders and hope that she won't ask who Lilly is. Because I have no idea.

The boy behind the counter heads towards me. 'Leon', his name badge says.

'I haven't seen you before,' he says and raises his eyebrows.

I have never cared about a boy's eyebrows before. Never considered that they can be ugly or attractive. His are dense, narrow and dark and follow an unusually perfect curve above is smiling eyes.

'I don't like coffee,' I explain, dragging my gaze from his eyebrows.

'Well then, you can't have tried my coffee,' says Leon.

He gives a relaxed smile, then quickly rattles through some barista secrets that I don't follow. His voice is as dark as the winter evening outside and makes my back feel clammy. My attempt to turn towards Selma is only halfway successful. A drop of sweat tickles my chest. Oh my God, just don't let sweat patches show through my shirt.

'Did you… take the pictures?' I try, nodding towards the wall.

'Yes, with a drone. I bought it with what I earned here last year.'

'Okay.'

'Yep. I'm going to study drone technology when I finish school. Come back before closing time tomorrow and I'll let you fly it,' he says. 'I'll make us some coffee to take with us.'

It wasn't a question. The world spins. My cheeks are glowing and I can feel sweat breaking out on my forehead too. The words I mean to say trip over each other before they reach my mouth. 'I have to…'

'Yes, she would love to,' Selma interrupts. She grabs my hand and pulls me towards the exit. From the door she shouts over her shoulder, 'Bring cinnamon swirls, they're her favourite!'

Then we hurry out into the dark.

The high street is empty. The rain has cleared up, but the air is still heavy with humidity. I button up my coat and walk faster than usual.

White light from the street lamps and shop windows is reflected in the puddles on the asphalt. Selma walks straight through them, as usual, while I dodge sideways to avoid the water. Even so, it seeps through the shoe leather and my socks are wet after a few steps.

I turn into a narrow, unlit side road. Selma follows just behind me, I can hear her breath.

'Wait!' she says and catches my arm.

We stop.

'I have no idea what happened,' I stutter. 'Of course I'm not going to meet up with him.'

'You have to. He's incredibly hot,' answers Selma. Her voice is calm again now. A bit too calm. 'And he likes taking pictures, just like you.'

Her face is blacked out in the shadow cast by a big container lorry. When I take a step towards her she backs further into the night.

'But it's *you're* the one in…'

'Yeah, but you're the one he wants to meet. I'll find someone else to stalk,' answers Selma. She clears her throat, leans forward and kisses me quickly on the cheek. 'Anyway, I'm so sick of coffee.'

Friday, 13th February.

'Where are you? Miss you, babe!'

The messages make my blood pump through my body a little harder. I smile. Just as I'm about to answer Leon the bus to the city centre approaches round the bend. I sit down at the back while Selma shows the driver the fake ticket on her phone. It's actually just a website made to look like a ticket.

'Why aren't you answering?' Leon writes, followed by a winking emoji.

Selma thumps down on the seat next to me with a

contented smile. She is wearing purple eye-liner, a checked coat and carries a bag which clinks. It's the sound of a party. As the bus turns onto the main road, she plucks the vodka bottle out of her bag and raises it to her glistening lips. She holds it out to me. I shake my head.

'Leon doesn't like it when girls get really drunk. So I thought I wouldn't drink too much.'

'How about this?' asks Selma, opening her handbag a crack so I catch a glimpse of a tobacco tin. The lid is half-way off and reveals a little bag of hash.

'When did you get into that?' I wonder.

Selma shrugs her shoulders. And I shake my head. We drive into a tunnel and the bus is filled with flashing orange lights. It's a regular Friday night.

Leon calls me for the third time as we are ringing the doorbell to his flat. Seconds later he's in the doorway in his black leavers' jumper. The bass from the sound system pulses out towards us.

'At last!'

The intensity of his smile and his deep blue eyes hit me like a massive wave. He thinks I'm gorgeous. I know he does, because I'm wearing the skirt and top he bought me. His arms creep decidedly around my waist. As he presses against me, I feel the lulling warmth of his body.

'You're here at last. Who were you with earlier on?' he mumbles, pressing his lips to mine before I can reply that I've just been at home.

His cologne smells of fresh sea mixed with springtime earth.

'Get a room!' says Selma, tapping me on on the bum before she disappears into the flat and the mass of people.

The music gets louder as Leon leads me into the living room. He shouts as he introduces me as 'his girl' to all his friends. Most of them are in the last year of college, like him. The pride tickles me. Leon has chosen me, above any of the girls in his year!

'Wait here, I'm just going to grab a beer,' he says and disappears into the kitchen.

I stand still while everything around me moves. There are bodies dancing, kissing in the sofa, arms in the air, smoking on the balcony, popcorn flying, phones filming, laughter drowning in music. And a warm hand on my shoulder. I turn round abruptly.

'Didn't we do the same photography course?' asks a boy, shouting to drown out the music.

I recognise the blonde curls and the slightly wonky front teeth.

'Yes! Last summer?' I shout back.

He shows me his profile where he posts his pictures, it has over a thousand followers already. I nod, impressed.

'Do you want to try? Italian amarone – there's nothing better!

He hands over his glass, I accept and taste it. The drink leaves a bitter and burning sensation in my mouth.

'You should meet my friend, she loves Italy and…'

An arm winds itself around my stomach and interrupts the conversation. I laugh as Leon twirls me round like a ballerina.

'Leon, this is…' I start.

'Come here, babe,' he says and pulls me further into the living room.

When I looks back the boy from summer school is already gone.

'You look so fucking good tonight,' smiles Leon, brushing my fringe behind my ear. 'Are you having fun?'

I nod. There are never any awkward silences when we talk. When I stand close to him it's like the world is on the right track. Nothing can go wrong when his skin presses against mine.

'Good,' he smiles. 'But hey, don't drink out of random people's glasses… It doesn't look good.'

He kisses me as the shame shoots up my spine. I'm like a kid caught red handed scrumping apples. Why did I do that. A girl his age would never have shown herself up like that. I want to say sorry. That I didn't think it through. But then he runs his tongue over mine, and I let my eyes close. The warmth from his hands floats down my back and stops at my bottom. I open my eyes a sliver. At the other end of the room is Selma. Her eyes are glassy and fixed on us. I get a feeling she has been studying us for some time.

'Wait,' I mumble into Leon's cheek.

'Is everything okay?'

He kisses me down my neck, his fingers run through my hair. I can't do it. I can't resist. So I close my eyes again. I let insecurity, shame and pleasure mix together as everything else fades into the distance.

'Watch out!'

The yell ploughs through the room. Some one is pointing. In the next second the whole party is staring at the ceiling, where a white drone is flying in uncontrolled semicircles like an angry and confused wasp. Something which looks like a white scarf is caught up one one of the rotor blades. Leon gets in front of me. He looks around, trying to get a handle on the situation.

'But what...'

All at once the drone loses speed and falls through the air. For a moment it's on a collision course into the party. People scatter to avoid it, some pressing themselves against the walls. The unreal feeling, familiar from when Leon first asked me out, returns. A girl squeaks, as if the whole thing is entertainment. Suddenly the drone finds hidden reserves of energy and powers upwards. People look uncertainly at each other. Is this planned? A joke? Then the vessel swivels round and pitches steeply downwards. Straight towards a boy with eyes wide like scoops of ice cream, who has backed himself into a corner. His cry is swallowed by the music, when the drone is right by his face he closes his eyes and flails his arms in a panic. His beer bottle flies out of his hand and hits a bookshelf, I don't hear it smash, but I can see the bits of glass and the white foam spraying. Then I spot her again. Standing halfway up the stairs is Selma. She is staring, panic-stricken down at everything unfolding. In her hands she is clutching a remote control.

It's like being hit by a firmly compacted snowball, right in the stomach.

Everything that follows happens in record time. The boy's hand hits the drone, the music stops and the drone hits the wall with a crash. I hear a cry of pain and a loud 'fuck'.

The silence rises like a mountain. The world is put on pause. Then everyone starts shouting at the same time, the party transforms into a chaos of questions, yelling and confusion. Soon the boy is surrounded.

'Move back,' shouts Leon, pushing through.

The boy is staring at his hand, it's bleeding from a cut. Someone starts filming the girl tying a yellow scarf round the injured area.

'It was her!' a boy shouts.

He points towards Selma, who is frozen on the stairs. She is still white, knuckling the remote control.

The drone is lying like a plane-wreck on the floor. I realise now what's tangled in the rotor blades.

The party breaks up in record time. Fifteen minutes after the crash, corks and empty beer bottles, smashed plastic cups and crisp packets lay abandoned in the living room. Cool air blows in the front door, where the last guests are making their way out.

'Sorry, sorry...' repeats Selma. 'It was just supposed to be funny...'

'Destroying people's stuff is a sick form of humour!' hisses Leon. 'As is sending people to A&E!'

Selma turns to me. Her purple eyeliner is smeared and looks like the beginnings of a rash. She throws up her hands.

'It's Valentine's Day tomorrow and you're going to lose the bet and…'

'What bet?' Leon interrupts.

An angry, red wrinkle threads along his forehead. I feel tired, like I've been sitting an exam for several days straight.

'I have no idea,' I say and look at the floor.

I stay like that. Totally still. Not until I hear Selma's footsteps followed by the front door slamming do I look up. And discover that I'm crying.

'Your friend is bad news,' huffs Leon, shaking his head.

His arm tightens around my shoulders. We fall down onto the sofa and I press myself against him like a kitten.

'That chick has been sitting around the café for weeks, staring at people. She dresses like a colour-blind whore and is completely hyper. And those townie tattoos!' The words storm out of him. 'On top of all that, people say she lives in a foster home.'

'They are practically her parents,' I whisper weakly.

'You shouldn't hang out with her any more,' Leon say more mildly. 'She's not right. One day it will look bad for you.'

'Actually she's really nice,' I mumble.

But inside the uncertainty grows. Selma is more and more over the top. Is Leon right?

'Drop her,' repeats Leon and gets up.

It feels like being dragged under water.

Saturday, 14th February

On Valentine's day the clouds sprinkle the first snow of the year on the town. It's closer to midday than morning when I'm woken by the sharp light shining in through a wide gap in the curtains, and the sound of a text.

'Sorry about yesterday, I didn't mean to get angry. But I saved for ages to afford that drone. And your friend irritates me. Come here at six – we can get some food and watch a film!'

Leon has sent a picture of himself lying in his bed with an innocent smile and warm eyes framed by long, black lashes and the beautiful eyebrows I noticed the first time we met.

Selma hasn't made a peep. She's not online anywhere either. Her last sign of life is a blurry video posted over night. She is sitting in a back-seat with some boys from the party. They are passing round a joint and there is lots of excited yelling as the speedometer hits 100km/hour.

The air in the room is stuffy. I don't know what I'm going to do. My head hits the pillow and I watch the video one more time. I can hear Selma's shrill yells through the speakers. She can make everyone believe that she is as happy as a lottery winner. But I can hear the underlying disturbance in the high pitched tones.

I fall asleep with my phone in my hand and dream that I am inside the computer game that Ulrik was playing, exactly one year ago. Then Leon's drone appears, airborne, and takes pictures of me. When I wake up I am starving and confused. But while I admire the snowflakes whirling, aimless, on the other side of the window, I make up my mind.

First of all I need to check my bank balance.

The heavy snowfall means the bus journey is twice as long.

'Where are you, cutie? Are you close yet?' Leon texts.

Through the window I can see a station wagon which has skidded off the road. Orange emergency lights are flashing. A car has stopped just behind it and a women in a hi-vis vest is heaving towing equipment out of the boot.

The clock on the panel at the front of the bus reads 17:50. I swing my legs, restless, I'm going to be late. The traffic creeps onwards.

Am I going to regret this?

When the bus at last turns into the station, I am already waiting ready at the doors. In a few minutes the town hall clock will chime six o'clock. Cold snow sticks to my face while I run through town and I regret choosing my high-heeled boots.

I stop in front of the electrical goods shop.

'Where are you? Answer me, babe. Miss you!' texts Leon.

I dry my face with my woollen scarf. Carefully, so as not to ruin my make up. Just then I am certain I have made the right choice. I push the door open with both hands and stride in. I pass shelves and displays full of robotic vacuum cleaners, huge TV screens, computers and cameras. Luckily there is no queue for the till. Just one single man, waiting to pay.

'Selma!'

My friend is behind the counter in a blue shirt and is about to out his goods in a paper bag. She looks up, surprised: 'What are you doing here?'

'This stupid day is damn important to you, right?' I yell.

The baker at the Italian restaurant throws the thin pizza bases up in the air before he cooks them in a huge stone oven. When the pizzas arrive at our table they are covered in piping hot pepperoni, fresh basil and cheese with a golden crust. Selma flirts with the waiter, he flirts back, and we order strawberry gelato for dessert. The knot of anxiety inside me unwinds gradually and disappears.

Afterwards we watch a classic Italian film, *Cinema Paradiso*, at a little cinema I didn't even know existed before I searched online earlier in the day. The film is black and white and just as boring as I expected, but Selma is engrossed and even laughs a couple of times.

'Unfortunately I didn't manage to hire any Vespas,' I say as we stroll out into the February evening after the screening. The snow has settled like white icing over the town.

Selma hems, curtly. Then she gets serious.

'Hey… A lot of shit has happened these last few weeks.'

'It's okay,' I say. 'You don't have to explain.'

'No, you deserve an explanation. You're my best friend.'

It feels like I'm being wrapped in a thick, protective woollen blanket.

'There have been arguments at home,' Selma continues. 'I failed some tests, almost lost my job because I swapped so many shifts... Then you got together with Leon. I thought I was fine with it... Anyway, I screwed up. You didn't have to do this.'

'In stormy weather, when you drive off the road, you need someone to tow you back on track,' I answer. 'And actually I think I like you even more when you screw up.'

'Does Leon hate me?'

I shrug. 'Wouldn't matter if he did.'

For a fleeting moment Selma looks shy, like a little girl. Then she straightens her back and quickly runs her hand through her black hair.

'Sisters before misters,' she says.

'Something like that,' I mumble.

We walk under the orange light of the lamp posts, past the white cloaked trees, towards the bus station. Pale mist rises up from the clumps of people waiting by the platforms.

'So. About that bet,' I begin.

We stop by a pole mounted with timetables. I open my back and fish out the bra Selma hung from the drone at the party yesterday, and pass it over to her.

'I won.'

• • •

'The Bet' was commissioned by students from the upper secondary schools of Haugaland, Kopervik, Skeisvang and Vardafjell in Norway.

ABOUT THE AUTHOR

Annette Münch is an author, journalist and copywriter from Oslo, Norway. She has edited youth magazines and has eighteen years of training in various martial arts.

Her debut novel, *The Chaos Warrior,* received the Ministry of Culture debut prize.

When writing *Girl Code,* she interviewed previous members of criminal and violent female gangs.

When writing *Badboy: Steroid,* she interviewed young men using anabolic steroids. The book was awarded several literary prizes.

Münch has also written a thriller, *Dropout,* and a non-fiction book about martial arts.

Rock 'n' Roll, baby!

Arne Svingen

Translated from Norwegian by Nancy Langfeldt

'This was not meant to be,' said Emile. 'You have a girl-friend, I have a boyfriend. We live almost 500 kilometres apart. It's not going to work.'

'You know, the first time you meet someone is like the opening track of an album,' said Jacob. 'You put the hit at the start, right? That's why it's track number two that really counts. If that song holds up you can relax and look forward to the rest of the record.'

Emile cocked her head to one side and looked at him for a long time. 'But there can't be a track number two for us.' Jacob nodded, resigned.

'I know,' he said, so quietly it was only just audible over the other voices in the café.

'But it was really nice to get to know you a little bit,' she said.

'And you, as well.'

She smiled at him. He smiled back. They hugged.

And then she was gone forever.

At least, that had been the plan. But now he's standing outside a whitewashed house in a strange town, freezing. He's been sitting on the train regretting it. And feeling excited. And scared. Whichever way he looks at it, there is just one conclusion: he has to take the risk. He might end up as the world's biggest idiot or he might just find he's made the smartest decision of his life so far. Because some meetings like that are not just sweet music. They are also an incredibly catchy hook that sticks to your brain.

That is why he is standing beneath a huge birch, looking into a well-lit living room. Inside, nothing is stirring. Nothing has happened in the hour he has been here. But he has plenty of time.

Suddenly he sees a shadow pass the window. A second later she appears at the next pane. She pauses, as if she is pondering something, before she disappears out of sight.

Emilie is home. That is half of the information he needs. Are her parents home too? What if her boyfriend is visiting?

He is patient. But only up to a point. That's why he

eventually plods over to the door, feeling a little dizzy, and presses on the doorbell.

Nothing happens.

He often plays his music so loud that he can't hear the doorbell, his mobile, or people throwing stones at his window. He walks up the stairs to hold down the doorbell, when suddenly the door opens.

'Oh?' she says, just half a metre away.

He was not expecting her to say anything sensible. Even with her hair up, wearing an old T shirt, she is more beautiful than he remembers.

'I have my guitar with me. And an amp,' he explains.

She looks at neither the guitar nor the amplifier, but behind him, as if she is expecting a full band.

'What are you doing here?' she asks.

'I couldn't just leave it.'

'You could have text me. Or rung.'

'You would have just told me not to come.'

'And what exactly is supposed to happen now?'

'I've written a song… for you. And I would really like to play it… to you.'

It's like putting a Spotify playlist on shuffle – he has no idea what's going to happen. The only thing he asks is that her silence is soon revealed to be a good thing.

'Oh my god, Jacob. Have you come all the way here to play a song for me?'

'Can I come in?'

She dithers, then takes a step back and makes clumsy hand gesture. There won't be a hug. He hadn't expected her to throw herself around his neck either. He just hoped that she wouldn't slam the door in his face.

Jacob is not sure if he should take off his jacket and shoes, or just plug in right there in the hallway. They look at each other. He can happily stand there for a while.

'Let's go down to the basement,' she says, and walks ahead through the kitchen and over to a dark staircase.

He bashes the amplifier into the door frame on the way down. She asks him to be careful.

Downstairs, Emile sits on the sofa. Jacob remains standing.

'What are you up to, exactly?' she asks.

'I have listened to the best songs in the world.'

'What are you talking about?'

'All the really good songs are about… stuff that is really hard to say, and much easier to sing about.'

'Feelings?'

Jacob nods.

'Also the lyrics say that you should take chances, or you'll end up regretting it forever.'

'So your life is some kind of pop song?'

'No, but the best lyrics tell you more in three minutes than a whole book can. It's not rock 'n' roll to stay at home and dream about everything that could have happened. You have to get out. Take the risk. Be a bit… naked. And I believe that's what I have done today. Except… with clothes.'

Emile smiles briefly.

'I have thought about you,' she says. 'It was actually

really nice to meet you... back then.'

Jacob puts down the guitar case and amplifier. The sofa is just a couple of steps away but even so he heads sideways and sits on the armrest of the wing-back chair.

'But I have a boyfriend,' she adds with a more serious expression. 'And you have a girlfriend?'

'There are a lot of songs about how good it is to have a boyfriend or girlfriend. People write about love all the time. But you know what?'

'Now I'm curious...'

'If not for some of the most beautiful songs in existence, a lot of people would just be with someone all right, someone okay, the best person they could find at the time. But the very best songs tell me that I can find something a hell of a lot better. Someone who is totally, totally... yeah, who's just...'

'Those songs will always tell you that you can find someone better. I wouldn't be good enough either after a while.'

'The difference is that I have written a song for you. And I have never done that for anyone else.'

Emilie's eyes narrow.

'And now you think that I'm going to fall for you the moment you play it? Like all girls just melt when they see a boy with a microphone or a guitar on a stage. Those songs tell you that, too, right? Write a song for a girl, and she will love you forever. That's cheap, Jacob.'

'But I think we have something totally special which...'

'The songs tell you that a single, short meeting in a

197

café is enough, right? The quick conversation we had has somehow made you sure that I am the one?'

'You did say you'd thought about me.'

Her face softens.

'I have.'

On the train he'd imagined hundreds of scenarios. None of them similar to this one. She has thought about him. No one says that unless those thoughts have taken up a lot of space.

'Before I met you, I didn't understand why everyone wanted to write about love,' Jacob explains, regretting it as soon as the words are out.

'So now you've started writing this gloop too?'

'Can I play you… my gloop?' Jacob asks, nodding at the equipment.

'Do I have a choice? You spent several hours on a train just to perform it.'

Jacob opens his guitar case and takes out the Stratocaster. He plugs in the cable and turns on the amplifier. The volume is already set to suit a performance without a microphone.

He starts in A and doesn't even need to think to find the frets. Then he starts singing. The acoustics are good down here, and he easily finds the tune. First he focuses out into the room, but soon his eyes land on Emilie, hunting for her reaction, a flicker of a positive response. She sits still with tight shoulders and face that's carved in marble.

The lines reveal just enough and are the best he has ever constructed. At the end of the last verse he feels the emotion rising up in him, a lump in his throat that threatens to choke his voice, but luckily he floats over to the chorus and finds some peace in the right chords. He doesn't even give in to the temptation to play the chorus a few extra times, just finishes the track as planned and lets the last G hang in the air until the sound settles.

The silence after good songs sometimes feels painful and sad. He doesn't mean to stare at her, but can't help if as he searches for a smile.

'It was…' she starts, but she takes a far too long and serious pause. 'You know, it wasn't really my type of music.'

'Okay.'

'And I didn't really follow the lyrics.'

'Maybe I didn't sing loud enough.'

'I'm sorry, it just wasn't my thing.'

'No worries.'

'No one has ever written a song for me, so I would love to have liked it. But…'

'Each to their own.'

'Yes, that's it. Sorry.'

'I… Yeah I should maybe…' says Jacob, pointing at the stairs.

'I can check the train times?'

'No, I can find out myself. If there is a long wait I'll find a café.'

Jacob unplugs the cable and puts the guitar in its case. Soon after he is outside the front door with the amplifier in one hand and the guitar in the other. It is totally impossible to give her a hug.

'I'm sorry,' Emilie repeats.

'It happens,' says Jacob, smiling carefully at her.

'Are you okay?'

'Yes, I am actually totally fine.'

'Are you? Okay. Goodbye then.'

She closes the door. But Jacob doesn't stop smiling. The best songs absolutely are not about the girl you get. The world's best songs are about heavy, all-consuming heart break. He strides towards the station. In his head is whole new hook.

· · ·

'Rock 'n' Roll, baby!' was commissioned by students from the upper secondary schools of Haugaland, Kopervik, Skeisvang and Vardafjell in Norway.

ABOUT THE AUTHOR

Arne Svingen left his job in 1997 to try to become an author. He published his first book two years later and since this debut has become one of the few Norwegian writers to have written and published a hundred novels.

He has received the Brage Prize, the Norwegian Culture Department's prize, along with many other awards. His books are translated into 20 languages and many of his books have been adapted for the screen.

The combination of humour and sincerity characterise his novels. *The Song of a Broken Nose* brought him his international breakthrough, and he is responsible for many popular series such as the thriller series *Svingen's Dark World* and the comic series *Svingen's Crazy World*. In 2019, his first stories about the child agent Elvin Griff appeared.

Arne Svingen has worked for several years to improve children and young people's reading skills, especially focusing on the reading abilities of boys. He is also responsible for the podcast *The Book World of Arne Svingen*, where he interviews other Norwegian authors writing children's books and their illustrators.

Frost Damage

Geir Tangen

Translated from Norwegian by Nancy Langfeldt

I stay in the background.

Out of sight, hidden behind wizened foliage and scrub. The naked branches claw out new, anxiety-filled paths in me. I raise my head up every now and then, to see if she's standing there. I'm scoping her house out, like I've been doing for several days now, waiting for a sign of life. Anything. A shadow on the window. A door jammed open. An open window that was shut the day before.

I know she is in there today, because I saw her. I saw her in the early hours of this morning, when she still had traces of sleep on her face. Her hair was untidy and she had a loose knot around the middle of her black kimono. I remember the feel of the silky soft fabric against my fingers like it was yesterday. Just like I remember everything else. The tender warmth when she held me close to her. Her burning skin against my cheek. The mischievous smile that always started as a twitch at edges of her mouth. Her soft lips, whispering in my ear. Her hands, carefully stroking my hair.

It's all so long ago. But at the same time it's no more than a breath between two heart beats away. It was just her and me. Two damaged people, united against the rest of the world. And now to end up here, on the outside of everything, concealed from curious eyes and watching her life carry on… It feels like I'm beneath contempt.

But I can't make that claim. She's not the one who left. It was me. She would have turned the world upside down to stop me if she could. But I couldn't be stopped. I was so completely tired of her. Tired of the needling and nagging. Tired of all the tears and the drama. Tired of her thinking she could boss me around. Tired of our arguments, and tired of her hysterics every time she didn't get her way. It didn't help that she said she loved me. She was a vulture, gnawing little pieces off me every day. I had to leave.

Sometimes I can trick myself into believing that this was inevitable. That we were oil and water. That it couldn't have ended differently. But that's not right either.

We would have made it if we'd put the effort in. If you try then at least you can wonder why it didn't work out despite all your efforts. It didn't help that we loved each other more than life itself. That we would both have gladly have run through a blazing inferno to save the other. We clung to each other through thick and thin, but when the everyday came creeping across the cold floor tiles, love just wasn't enough.

The frost bites my jaw. It hammers on sensitive nerves, which scream for my attention. But I feel nothing. All I can see is her sitting room, through the window at the front. It's warm in there – there's condensation on the glass and everything inside casts long, flickering shadows around the room. Ice crystals are forming on the blades of grass between my fingers. I have to arch my back and lift my head to see past the bare bushes I am crouching behind. I've lost count of the number of times I've been stationed at a lookout post like this. The number of times I've watched silent people through a scope. On the steep slopes of Djibouti, along the winding, muddy tracks of Eritrea, and in chaotic bomb craters in Syria. And now here I am in my home country, Norway. I put the world between us to get away from her, but I've always known that gravity would bring me right back. Love doesn't recognise land borders. It doesn't differentiate between good and bad, between the rational and the emotional. Love just is. Naked, honest and senseless.

At this hour there's little chance she will spot me out here. Looking out from a well-lit room into a dark land-scape, you're as likely to see what's outside as what's happening on the dark side of the moon. I gather my strength and raise my head a little higher.

The heavy oak tree leans on the easterly wall, and long dark branches stretch their arms towards the light. The night, like me, is on the outside wanting to get in. Into the warmth it knows is there. I gasp for breath when I see her get up from her chair and walk towards the window. She is just as beautiful as before. Her long dark hair frames her face and waves down over her shoulders. Through the scope she feels so close to me I can see her chest rise and fall, but she is still so very far away. Further now than when I shot my way to freedom from two months of imprisonment in Zambia. I can see her stretching towards the ceiling and rolling her neck. The longing to sink into her arms and forget everything bad is so intense that it feels like a physical pain in my chest.

I know it now. I know that I love her more than anything else. It's here with her that I belong. But she doesn't know it. She doesn't know I am out here in the frozen grass spying on her. I delay the inevitable and steal some small glimpses. No more than that. One or two seconds, that's all. A tiny fragment of time in which I feel whole. Miniscule grains of sand pass through an hourglass in the moments where good triumphs and I am returned to her. Everything that has happened is erased. Tears squeeze their way out when I see her standing there. She is alone, her arms at her sides. She is wearing a marine blue top, the first button undone. My eyes linger on her. I capture a new image to remember her by. I sense a melancholy air about her. Like she is also looking at something that used to exist, but was gone before its time.

If things had been different, I could stand up right now. Brush the snow off my field trousers and walk up to her door. Ring the bell, wait for her to open up. Be welcomed and invited in. But the way things happened, that wouldn't work out. The words I said will not disappear. I told her to go to hell. I said that I hated her and never wanted to see her ugly face again. I screamed and I lashed out. I spat out threats and ridiculed her, and laughed out loud when she cried. I turned my back and swore that I would never return.

Perhaps that's what love is like?

Back then I felt nothing but heartfelt disdain, but now, just four years later, the longing is a river whose current is stronger and stronger. I've realised that I can't live without her. She is everything to me. She just doesn't know it. Not yet.

Everything would be simpler if I could just say it. Tell her how I feel. Accept her curses and anger and then turn on my heel when she was finished. But I don't have the guts. I know I would hit rock bottom. I would lose my footing and fall. So it's best that I keep my distance.

The hours crawl towards the evening. I can see that she is restless. It's like she is waiting for someone. Someone who should have arrived some time ago. She gets up every time a car crunches over the gravel, looks out but turns her back when the car has passed. I have lost all feeling in my fingers and toes and I know that I should give up soon. My trousers, which were damp when I lay down in the grass, have stiffened in the frost and are burning my thighs. Just like yesterday and the day before that. I had her in my sights those evenings too, but was too cowardly in the last moments. The only thing bringing me back, night after night, is this eternal longing which has dug its way into me. It's made a deep, painful borehole, splintering bones and gristle along the way. The longing crushes me until I am just a silent scream howling out into the void.

It's the worst kind of self destruction. I know. I'm punishing myself. I'm paying the price, but I don't know if the punishment fits the crime.

I was the one who left. It was me who let her down. It was me who yelled all those ugly words, and told her to start again without me. It was me who trampled on everything she held dear and who burned all my bridges on the way out. What, if anything, is the appropriate punishment for all this? I don't know – that that's why I keep coming back. I lie here in the grass, frostbitten, with bronchitis, chilblains and a bladder infection. All to see her one more time. Just once more.

Endlessly beautiful. Endlessly kind. Endlessly dear… Everything about her seems to be endless. But still, that's not how it was. I wanted to tear myself away from her, but I could find no joy on my own. I thought I had chosen freedom, that I was breaking my chains by leaving. That the outside world had so much more to offer than she could give me. I know better now. It's been an expensive lesson. I had to get away from her to un-derstand that I loved her. I had to break away to understand that I had alway been free. The tears flow now, as I understand that I lost what was dearest to me by looking for something that I already had.

The moon settles just above the roof of the house and blinks down at me. He is a lonely soldier just like me. A scout who observes people. He looks down at the earth and shakes his head. The moon knows how little we understand.

I stare at him for a while, then I nod curtly and stand up. I leave the scope lying in the grass. I pick up the green military backpack which contains everything I own. Everything I've ever owned. My unsteady legs take me, faltering, towards the house. One step at a time. I grip my backpack tightly – it's the final link. It anchors me to the life I have lived. To the foreign legion. To the dead souls clawing at my brain in the night. I straighten up my uniform. I tuck my beret under my arm. I keep myself hidden behind the hedge that surrounds the garden like a wreath. Then I sneak closer, sheltered by the oak, knowing that the frost crunching beneath my boots can't be heard from the bay window.

Where this courage has come from I don't know. Maybe my hopelessness is driving me. Something happened inside me when I was lying there, looking up at the moon. Whether it was something giving way or something sticking me back together is hard to say. Whatever it was, it's pushing me towards the door. The same door I have stood before so many times.

I'm breathing heavily. I hold onto a post to keep myself

upright. My heart is hammering against my ribs and my thoughts tumble round in my head, unable to settle down. My finger shakes as I press the doorbell. I can hear the bells chime their way through the hall. It's totally quiet outside. My frosty breath condenses on the window pane in the door. The droplets start to freeze and gather into streams. I blink again and again. I'm terrified but somehow I feel safe. It couldn't carry on like this. At some point it had to end.

After a while the door opens and there she is. A few years older. Apart from that, it's as if time has stood still. Her eyes snap open and she claps her hands to her face. I can hear her gasping for breath. Then she lowers her hands and I can see tears glittering in her eyes. Saying nothing, she comes towards me. She opens her arms and embraces me. It's like the channel has cracked open, and I can see a way through when before it was frozen over. I breath in the scent of her perfume. It's the same one I bought her for Christmas, many years ago.

'My god… Is that you, Arvid? Is it really you?'

I want to stay in her arms. I don't want to let go. I just want to feel her warm hands defrosting me. Inside and out. First I say nothing. The words can't find their way out, but at last I manage to whisper. I stroke her back, kiss her cheek. And whisper the words which have been on my mind every single day since I left her, three years, thirty weeks, four days and two hours ago.

'Yes, it's me, Mamma… I have missed you.'

• • •

'Frost Damage' was commissioned by students from the upper secondary schools of Haugaland, Kopervik, Skeisvang and Vardafjell in Norway.

ABOUT THE AUTHOR

Geir Tangen was born in 1970 and published his first crime novel, *Maestro*, in 2016. He has published two more crime novels in the same series: *Heartbreaker* in 2017 and *Dead Man's Tango* in 2018. The publishing rights to his two first novels have been sold to fifteen countries, while his last book has been sold to Denmark, Italy, Netherlands, Sweden and Germany. He has also written some short stories for anthologies.

As well as being a successful author, he works as a teacher in Haugesund, Norway.

ABOUT THE TRANSLATORS

Nancy Langfeldt is a British/Norwegian literary translator. She moved to the UK to study Engish Literature at the University of York and has remained here since, making Birmingham home for the past ten years. In 2015 Nancy completed a mentorship under translator Don Bartlett through the British Institure of Literary Translation. In addition to translating she works at Loaf Community Bakery and Birmingham Bike Foundry, two worker co-operatives in the city.

Beth Fowler was born in 1980, in Inverness. She studied Hispanic Studies at the University of Glasgow, spending time in Chile and Portugal as part of her course. She has been a translator since 2009, working from Portuguese and Spanish to English. In 2010, she won the Harvill Secker Young Translators' Prize and shortly afterwards was commissioned to do her first book-length translation, *Open Door*, by Iosi Havilio (And Other Stories, 2011). Since then she has had a further three novel translations published: *Paradises,* also by Iosi Havilio (And Other Stories, 2013), *Ten Women*, by Marcela Serrano (Amazon Crossing, 2014) and *We All Loved Cowboys*, by Carol Bensimon (Transit Books, 2018). She lives near Glasgow with her husband and two children.

ABOUT THE ILLUSTRATOR

Riya Chowdhury is an illustrator based in the West Midlands who likes to experiment with different mediums, including traditional and digital. She is interested in fantasy and science fiction themes but likes to challenge her skills and work outside of her comfort zone.

See more of her work here: www.ri-ya.co.uk

Spark
Young Writers

Creative writing groups for children and young people in the West Midlands

£90 per year
£9 per session
Aged 8–17

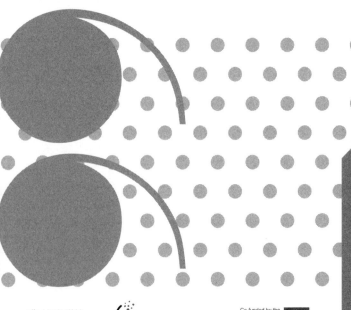

writingwestmidlands.org